wondergirls ™

"And the Winner Is..."

Jillian Brooks

SCHOLASTIC INC.

New York Toronto London Auckland Sydney
Mexico City New Delhi Hong Kong Buenos Aires

ISBN 0-439-35492-7

Copyright © 2002 17th Street Productions,
an Alloy, Inc. company
All rights reserved.
Published by Scholastic Inc.

 Produced by 17th Street Productions,
an Alloy, Inc. company
151 West 26th Street
New York, NY 10001

12 11 10 9 8 7 6 5 4 3   2 3 4 5 6 7/0

Printed in the U.S.A.   40
First Scholastic printing, September 2002

chapter
ONE

Who, ME?????
Yes, YOU Can Make a Difference!
Run for Class Office at WLMS! Get Your
Applications in NOW to the
Student Government Room.
Election Day is Oct. 15!

"Heads up!"

I ducked as a fast-flying object whirled past my head and crash-landed on the school lawn.

"Oops, sorry about that," a boy called. He jogged up and gave me a crooked grin. "Max was supposed to catch it back there."

"No problem," I said. I stooped to pick up the Frisbee and threw it back to Max, who was standing sheepishly a few feet away. The heavy knapsack on my shoulder slipped, nearly knocking me off balance. This morning was not starting off well.

1

Max, a tall skinny boy with glasses, missed again. I shrugged. "Bad throw, I guess," I said.

"Well. Thanks, anyway," the first boy told me. He gave another crooked grin, then ran back toward his friend. "You're a total loser, Wexel!" he shouted.

"Good morning, Amanda," a voice said cheerfully. *Way* too cheerfully. "Guess you're awake now!"

I turned to find one of my three best friends, Traci McClintic, standing beside me. She was wearing jeans and a Wonder Lake Muskrats Soccer T-shirt. Traci recently moved to our town from Charleston, South Carolina. She and one of my other best friends, Arielle Davis, are both amazing soccer players.

"Hey, Trace," I said. "How's it going?"

"Just great," Traci replied. "Fantastic. Amazingly well. Don't you remember what today is?"

"No," I admitted. I bit my lip. Was it Traci's birthday or something? Was there some special event at school? I couldn't remember making any notes in my day planner about it, and I keep track of *everything*. "Um . . . Thursday?" I tried.

Traci frowned. "Well, yeah," she said. "But it's also Un-grounding Day! How could you forget?"

"Oh, right!" I smacked myself on the forehead. "Sorry."

Just then I spotted our two other best friends, Arielle Davis and Felicia Fiol, heading toward us. We'd all been grounded by our parents for two whole

2

weeks. We'd gotten into a little bit of trouble with a plan to break up my baby-sitter and Felicia's dad, but I didn't really want to think about that right now.

Felicia was practically dancing with glee, her long dark hair bouncing on her shoulders. "We're free, we're free!" she cried, twirling around with her arms in the air.

Arielle, looking perfect as usual, her auburn hair cut in the latest style and the pleats in her short plaid skirt neatly pressed, glanced around at the crowd of Wonder Lake Middle School students on the lawn. "Felicia, quit that," she said in a low voice. "You're making us all look stupid."

Felicia immediately straightened up and stopped jumping. "Sorry," she said.

"Hey, I feel like acting a little crazy, too," Traci said. "Those were the longest two weeks of my life! No TV, no E-mail, no phone, no going out." She shuddered. "And my weird brother kept popping into my room every five minutes just to bug me."

I smiled. "Hey, Dave's not that bad." Traci's brother was thirteen, two years older than us, and an eighth grader at Wonder Lake Middle School. True, he *did* act a little goofy sometimes. But he was also really nice. And really cute, too, with the same light blond hair and freckles as Traci.

"That's what *you* think," Traci said. "You don't have to live with him."

"Well, anyway, we probably did sort of deserve to be grounded," I pointed out. "It wasn't very nice of us to try and break up Penny and Felicia's dad." Penny, a really cool young artist, is my part-time baby-sitter. Really, she's more like a friend. I'm way too old to have a baby-sitter, but she helps take care of my twin stepbrother and sister, Jessy and Joey. Lately Penny had started dating Mr. Fiol, which didn't make either me or Felicia very happy. We had pulled a nasty prank to sort of scare Penny away from Mr. Fiol, but it had backfired. Badly. And now I had to admit, it had been pretty terrible of us in the first place.

Felicia sighed. "Let's just forget about all of that for now, okay?"

"Being grounded wasn't so bad for me, actually," Arielle said as we began to move toward the front steps of the school. "At least I got to make a few emergency trips to the mall."

Traci's mouth dropped open. "You *did?*" she said. "You lucky duck. How'd you manage that?"

Arielle shrugged. "I just know how to manage my parents, that's all. You have to ask at exactly the right time, when they're not really paying attention. The first time I told them I needed some new notebooks. The next time I told them I had to buy the class present for a special teacher's birthday."

"Which teacher?" Traci asked suspiciously.

Arielle grinned. "Ms. McClintic, of course."

Traci threw up her hands. "*My* mom? I can't believe it! How could you say that? Her birthday's not until July!"

"Well, she was the first person I thought of," Arielle said. "She *does* teach music at Wonder Lake. And she's our homeroom teacher, too. It was perfect."

Behind Arielle's back, I threw Traci a sympathetic smile. The McClintics had moved to Wonder Lake just before school started, so I hadn't known her for very long. But I'd been best friends with Arielle since pre-K, so I knew Arielle like a book. She never failed to come up with an instant plan—usually a good one—for any situation.

"So what else did you guys do while you were grounded?" Felicia asked as we entered the big, crowded school lobby. The first bell hadn't rung yet, so students were hanging out in groups, laughing and comparing notes on the weekend. "We didn't get to talk much for the last two weeks. Hanging out at school just isn't the same."

"I practiced that dumb clarinet piece for orchestra," Traci grumbled. She held up her black instrument case as evidence. "Over and over and over again. Mom's orders." Then she brightened. "It did bug Dave, though. A lot."

"I spent some quality time with Jessy and Joey," I told my friends. My little stepsister and brother are

5

four years old and twin terrors. "My stepmom was helping crabby old Great-aunt Delores move."

"Why didn't Penny baby-sit them?" Traci asked.

I carefully adjusted the strap on my purple denim overalls. "Um, Penny's been really busy, I guess. She's got this amazing new sculpture she's working on at the studio, and she's, uh . . ." I glanced at Felicia. "Going out more."

Felicia sighed. "I know. With my dad. I still can't believe it." Felicia's parents had been divorced for a while, but Penny was the first woman Mr. Fiol had dated so far. Felicia's mom owned Fiol's Bakery in the town square and lived in an apartment above the store. I had no idea whether Mrs. Fiol was dating anyone, but I sure didn't want to ask Felicia. It would be totally rude.

"Well, I helped out a lot at the bakery," Felicia went on. She rummaged in her knapsack and pulled out a glossy teen magazine. "And I started this no-fail home fitness program. All you need is a mat and your favorite CDs. Check it out."

Traci peered over Felicia's shoulder. "Ugh," she said. "Sit-ups and stretches."

"We have to do those all the time in soccer practice," Arielle said, with a wave of her hand. "No big deal."

Felicia looked a little hurt. "Well, it says here that—"

Suddenly someone pushed into Traci, knocking

her into Felicia. "Sorry," Traci told her, frowning. She whirled around just in time to see Ryan Bradley, a boy from our sixth-grade class, heading toward homeroom with two of his friends.

"Ooo-la-la, so sorry. *Pardonnez-moi*, Dixie Chick," Ryan called over his shoulder in a high, ridiculous French accent. He's always teasing Traci. You'd almost think he had a crush on her.

Traci's face flamed red. "I hate it when he calls me that," she said under her breath. "I'll see you guys later, okay?" She pushed her way down the hall after Ryan.

Arielle snorted. "Oh, puh-leeze," she said. "Those two are so obvious. Why don't they just admit they like each other and start dating?"

"My dad says no dates for me until high school," Felicia said with a sigh.

Arielle looked shocked. "Really? Well, don't worry, we'll get him to change his mind." Then she turned to me. "Speaking of dating, how are you and Davey-boy doing?"

"Dave? You mean, Traci's brother?" I started walking quickly down the hall. "I don't know what you're talking about."

Arielle hurried after me, with Felicia close behind. "Come on, Amanda, you guys are as bad as Traci and Ryan. Believe me, I know a crush when I see one."

I frowned. "Arielle, that's the dumbest thing I ever heard."

7

Arielle smiled knowingly. "Oh, really? What's the matter, are you afraid Traci will be mad?"

I stopped short in the middle of the crowded hallway. "Look, this is just a stupid subject, and I don't feel like talking about it right now. I have to go to my locker, okay? See you in homeroom."

"Whatever you say, Amanda Panda," Arielle said sweetly, using the nickname she'd given me in first grade. She waggled her fingers and kept walking down the hall.

"Bye, Amanda," Felicia said. "Guess I'd better get going, too. See you at lunch, okay?" Felicia's homeroom was in a different part of the building.

"Yeah, sure," I answered. "See you later." I went over to my locker and began to spin the combination lock, feeling totally relieved that I didn't have to listen to any more of Arielle's crazy comments about Dave McClintic. Yeah, Dave was cute. And funny. And sweet, even if Traci didn't think so. I liked the way he always seemed kind of shy and tongue-tied. But that didn't mean I actually had a *crush* on him. Did it?

"Hey. It's Amanda, right?"

I looked up. Oh, wow. I couldn't believe it. Asher Bank, the supercute student council president, an eighth grader, was leaning against the locker next to mine.

I was so startled that I completely missed the last number of my combination. "Um, hi," I replied, trying to sound casual. "What's up?"

"Not too much," Asher said. "I'm glad I ran into you, though."

"You are?" I said. Then I wanted to kick myself. I sounded so dumb, so . . . sixth grade. Asher was just a guy. No big deal.

Asher pushed a hand through his wavy dark hair and smiled. I couldn't help noticing how his brown eyes kind of crinkled up.

"Well, yeah," Asher said. "I wanted to thank you for coming to our first student government meeting last week. You really had some good ideas, you know?"

"I did?" I said, before I caught myself. Now I sounded even dumber, if that was possible. "I mean, well, thanks." I racked my brain for exactly what it was I'd said at the meeting. Usually I remember stuff like that. Asher was going to think I was a total space case.

Just then Arielle hurried up to us, frowning. "Amanda, come *on*." She tugged on my sleeve, but soon her eyes were glued on Asher. "Hi," she said, smiling a megawatt smile at him. "I'm Arielle. Aren't you the guy from student government?"

"Yeah, I'm Asher." Asher flashed a megawatt smile of his own. Gosh, he was cute. "Nice to meet you. Listen, I won't hold you guys up," Asher said quickly. "But hey, we really do need more smart, committed kids to become involved here at WLMS." He turned toward Arielle. "How about you, Arielle? Are you interested in student government, too?"

9

Arielle beamed. "Um, sure," she said, grinning at Asher. "I guess." I knew for a fact that Arielle thought student government was unbelievably boring, but I guess she also thought Asher was unbelievably cute. Suddenly three girls walked over and tapped Arielle on the shoulder. I knew they were on the soccer team, but I didn't know their names.

"Arielle?" one of the girls asked. "Hey, we have some questions for you about practice today."

Arielle looked less than thrilled to leave Asher, but she kept her cool. "Okay, then. Listen, I have to go. I guess I'll catch you guys later."

Asher nodded and waved. "Later," he called. Then he turned back to me and cleared his throat. "Well, anyway, Amanda, I'll get right to the point."

I looked at him in surprise. What was this all about? Asher wasn't about to . . . ask me out, was he? *No*, I told myself quickly. *He's probably the most popular guy at school.* Besides, I wasn't really interested in him that way. But why did he keep looking at me with that weird, intense stare?

"I was wondering if you might like to . . ."

I could not believe this was happening.

". . . run for sixth-grade class president."

Phew! I let out my breath in relief. Of course Asher wasn't asking me out! What had I been thinking? But class president? I loved taking part in student government, but I'd never thought about being class *president* before. It seemed like a huge responsibility.

"Gosh, I don't know," I replied. "I mean, I never really thought about anything like that."

"Well, maybe you should," Asher said. "I bet you'd be great. You know about how the school board is voting on cutting the arts budget?"

I groaned, thinking about it. There was a resolution being put before the school board to trim the arts budget and spend more on our championship-winning sports teams. It was kind of a weird issue with me and my friends, because I was totally into art, and Traci and Arielle were *so* into soccer. I was against cutting the arts budget, but I didn't think they were. "Sure," I said, looking at Asher. "What about it?"

Asher shrugged. "I just thought you seemed so convincing when you talked about it at our meeting. You're so passionate about the arts, I bet you'd make a great candidate."

I smiled and shook my head. "Wow, that's really nice of you. I don't know if I'm the leader type, but I'll think about it."

Asher just smiled. "Great."

I raised my eyebrows. Was this guy for real? But before I could reply, the bell on the wall above us rang sharply. We both held our ears.

"Guess we'd better get moving," Asher said when the bell finally stopped. "Cassandra Jackson and I

11

have to go around to the homerooms this morning, making a pitch for student government. I'll see you later, then?"

"Okay," I told him, shutting my locker. "I'll think about what you said."

chapter
TWO

From Amanda's notebook

<u>REASONS I SHOULD RUN</u>:
1. IMPORTANT TO BE INVOLVED!
2. ARTS PROGRAM (YAY!) VS. SPORTS PROGRAM (BOO!)
3. PUBLIC-SPEAKING EXPERIENCE
4. MEET NEW PEOPLE
5. LOOKS GOOD ON SCHOOL RECORD

<u>REASONS I SHOULDN'T RUN</u>:
1. NO MORE FREE TIME!!!
2. ARIELLE AND TRACI ARE TOTALLY INTO SPORTS
3. AM I REALLY POPULAR ENOUGH TO WIN?
4. ARIELLE THINKS ASHER BANK IS A BABE (PUH-LEEZ!) AND SHE'LL BE JEALOUS.

I made it into homeroom just as Ms. McClintic was about to shut the door.

"Right under the wire, Amanda," Traci's mom told me with a smile. "Must be your lucky day." She looked a lot like Traci, with her blond hair, brown eyes, and freckles. I thought Ms. McClintic was pretty cool for a teacher, even if she *was* a little ditzy.

I nodded breathlessly and quickly headed to my seat next to Arielle at the back of the room.

"Ooooo," Ryan Bradley said loudly as I passed. "It's a miracle. Kepner almost got in trouble."

Behind him, Traci gave his chair a kick.

I just ignored Ryan. The two of us are usually pretty good friends, but he can be really annoying sometimes. I had hardly put down my books and taken my seat before Arielle leaned across the aisle. "So, how do you know Asher Bank?" she asked.

"I don't," I said, shrugging. "Not really."

"I can't believe you were talking with him like that. He's only the coolest guy in the school," Arielle said. "And guess what? I heard he doesn't have a girlfriend this year. Yet."

I sighed. Arielle was always so boy crazy! It really bugged me sometimes. "Thanks for letting me know, Arielle, but I just don't care."

Arielle looked hurt.

Traci whirled around in her chair. "Care about what?" she asked.

"Just some gorgeous guy who's obviously crushing on her," Arielle said.

I could feel my face burning. "No way, Arielle," I told her. "You are so totally off base."

"I *know* when guys are interested," Arielle insisted.

"Look, Asher is *not* interested," I countered. "He was talking to me about student government, remember? You heard him."

"Oh," Arielle said, sounding disappointed. "That's it?"

"He wants me to run for sixth-grade class president," I said, frowning. "It's kind of nuts, huh?"

"I don't think it's nuts at all," Traci said with a grin. "You'd be a fantastic president, Amanda."

Arielle looked thoughtful. "Well, you'd have to get elected first. But I could help you get lots of votes."

"Gee, thanks," I said.

"No, I mean it," Arielle said. "Traci's right. You're the perfect candidate. After all, you're good at organizing stuff and getting things done. But what's so great about student government, anyway? The kids are all geeks."

"Like Asher Bank?" Traci said.

Arielle shrugged. "Well, okay. He's an exception. A *major* one."

I shook my head. Once Arielle makes up her mind about something, she never changes it. Even though I always say I know my best friend like a book, the truth is, sometimes I don't understand her at all. Back in grade school, I almost always agreed with Arielle on everything. If Arielle didn't think something was cool, I didn't do it. But we were in middle school now. Things were going to be different.

15

"I already signed up for student government last week," I reminded Arielle. "I just never thought about running for a class office."

Arielle tapped her chin with one lavender fingernail. "Well, you *could* probably win. All it takes is a positive attitude."

"So what exactly do you *do* in student government?" Traci asked.

"I've only been to one meeting," I said, "but you help run the school. You know, represent the students' opinions on stuff. Like . . ." I took a deep breath, glancing at my sports-loving friends. "Whether they should cut money from the arts program and put more into the sports program."

"Sounds like a no-brainer to me," Arielle said, shrugging.

I frowned at her. Sometimes Arielle says things without thinking first, and it really bothers me. "You've got to be kidding. You mean you really think they should give more money to sports than to arts?"

"Sure," Arielle said. "For one thing, our soccer team needs new uniforms."

"Um," Traci said under her breath. "Maybe we shouldn't get into this right now."

"Ladies," Ms. McClintic broke in from the front of the room, "would you like to fill us all in on what is so important back there?"

"No," Traci said quickly, twisting back in her chair.

"I believe I was talking," Ms. McClintic went on. "And I had asked for everyone's attention."

"Sorry," I mumbled, looking down at my desk. I hate getting scolded by teachers. It only seems to happen when I'm with Arielle.

"McClintic sure is grouchy today," Arielle whispered. "Hey, Traci, what's wrong with your mom?"

Traci's shoulders stiffened, but she didn't turn around.

"Shhh!" I warned Arielle. "Do you want to get us grounded again?"

"Anyway, as I was saying," Ms. McClintic continued, "we will have visitors to homeroom this morning. Some of the seventh- and eighth-grade class officers are going to tell us about the upcoming elections at WLMS. It would be very nice if you would all give them your *undivided* attention."

Arielle gave Ms. McClintic an angelic smile.

"Speaking of grounding," she said to me as Ms. McClintic walked over to her desk to find her attendance book. "What are we going to do first, now that we're finally free?"

I hesitated for a second. Everyone else in the class was talking now, so it was probably okay. Ms. McClintic didn't seem to mind. She was too busy searching her desk for the attendance book.

"Well, we should do *something*," I said finally. "We definitely need to celebrate."

Traci scribbled on an empty page at the back of her science lab notebook, tore it out, and folded it into a tiny square. Then she tossed it quickly over her shoulder.

The note landed on the floor in front of my foot. Carefully I stepped on the paper and drew it toward me. Ms. McClintic had finally found her book and was making her way through the roll. She didn't seem to notice.

"Bradley, Ryan?" Ms. McClintic called.

"Present," Ryan said. "I also accept gift certificates."

The whole class groaned.

"What does the note say?" Arielle whispered, craning her neck.

I turned the crumpled paper toward her.

Un-grounding party? My house after school. We can ask Felicia at lunch. T.

Traci glanced back over her shoulder. Arielle gave her a grin and a thumbs-up. "Excellent," she said. I just nodded happily. It felt great to be free again!

There was a knock at the classroom door. "Come in," Ms. McClintic said.

The door opened and Asher Bank entered, followed by a tall, dark-haired girl with funky black glasses.

"Hi, everyone," Asher said, glancing around the room. When he saw me, he smiled slightly.

"See?" Arielle whispered. "I told you he likes you."

"I give up," I said with a sigh. "You're hopeless, Arielle."

"Hi, guys. My name is Asher Bank, and I'm your student council president," Asher began.

The girl with the glasses stepped forward. "And I'm Cassandra Jackson, the seventh-grade president. Hi."

"Somebody could use a visit from the fashion police," Arielle said in a low voice.

"Shhh," I said, frowning. There was nothing wrong with Cassandra's outfit. Actually, I thought she looked pretty cool in her black jeans and long vintage sweater. Her black boots made her look even taller.

"As Ms. McClintic probably told you, we're here to talk to you about getting involved in student government," Asher continued. "I think some of you have already signed up." He smiled at me again. "But we still need a lot more people to get involved."

"And we also need kids to run for president, vice president, secretary, and treasurer for each class," Cassandra put in. "Elections will be in two weeks. All you have to do is sign up on the list in the student government office. Then get fifty names on a petition to put you on the ballot."

"Fifty?" Arielle whispered. "That's too easy."

I bit my lip. Fifty people was doable, especially with Arielle's help. But the campaign would take a lot of work—if I *did* decide to run.

19

"About a week from now, we'll have a debate between the candidates, just like the presidential debates on TV," Cassandra said. "And the day before the election, each candidate will give a speech."

The elections are only two weeks away, I thought. *That doesn't give much time to prepare for a debate. And a speech* . . . I shuddered. I'm the kind of person who likes to have everything perfectly organized and prepared, and it was sounding like I'd have my work cut out for me if I ran.

"So in the debate, the candidates get to argue a lot, right?" Ryan Bradley asked. "Cool."

Asher grinned. "Well, not exactly. It's more like a talk about the issues and backing up your opinions with facts."

"He's got a future in politics for sure," Arielle whispered. "Or wait a minute, maybe he could be a lawyer. He sounds just like my parents when they're talking about their cases at home."

Steve Perry, who had a white-blond buzz cut and always drew fake tattoos on his arm with a ballpoint pen, looked disappointed. "So you mean no one wins?"

"Well, kind of," Asher answered. "Each of you will get to decide for yourself who won. When you cast your vote."

"What kind of issues do you mean?" another boy asked. "Like, bad cafeteria food?"

That really bugged me. "There are lots more

20

important things to think about than that," I spoke up. "What about the budget cuts for the WLMS arts program?"

Everyone suddenly turned to stare at me, and I felt kind of weird. But then, I was kind of proud of myself for voicing my opinion. Would I be able to handle a debate for my campaign? I wasn't sure. *I don't know if I'm ready for this*, I thought.

"Well, that's a really good example," Asher said. "Each candidate has to decide what issues are most important. Then he or she decides how they feel about those issues and puts together their campaign."

"This is getting really stupid," Arielle muttered. She opened her Trapper Keeper and took out a piece of scrap paper. "Hey, Traci, want to play ticktacktoe?"

"Okay," Traci replied. "But I'm X. And I get to start."

I sighed. How could those two be so totally disinterested in what happened at their own school? What if the administration decided to cut soccer from the WLMS sports program? Would they care then?

A blond girl in the front of the room raised her hand. "What does the class secretary do?" she asked.

"We'll run down all the positions for you guys," Asher said. He and Cassandra explained the different responsibilities for president, vice president, secretary, and treasurer.

"Forget treasurer," Ryan spoke out. "I stink at

math. But maybe I could run for some other position. Like homework eliminator."

"How about class clown?" Traci said. But Ryan didn't seem upset by her comment. He actually looked kind of pleased.

The first-period bell rang just as Cassandra was about to tell us some of the special privileges of being a class officer.

"Saved," Arielle said under her breath, marking her third O in a diagonal row on the ticktacktoe board. "Too bad, Trace."

"Oh, dear," Ms. McClintic said. "I'm afraid we'll have to stop now. Thank you for coming by, Asher and Cassandra."

"No problem," Cassandra said. "Thanks for listening, everyone."

"And don't forget to sign up at the student government office," Asher added. He looked straight at me again. I tried to smile.

Arielle reached out and poked me with the eraser end of her pencil. I hate it when she does that. "I'm telling you," she said. "He likes you. It's so obvious."

"Ow," I said, rubbing my arm. "Quit it, Arielle." But my mind was on the whole run-or-not-to-run question. Should I give it a try? Was I ready for that kind of responsibility?

Kids had begun to gather their books together

and file out of homeroom. Arielle grabbed her Spanish notebook and made a beeline toward the door.

I quickly followed her, with Traci close behind. I didn't like the sudden determined look on Arielle's face. Whenever she got some sneaky idea, her eyes got really bright. What was she up to?

Arielle caught up to Asher, who had just stepped into the hall, and tapped him on the shoulder. "I know the perfect person to run for class president," she said.

"Uh, great," Asher said. Then he frowned slightly. "It's Arielle, right?" he said. "We met this morning."

Arielle looked pleased. "Yeah, that was me," she said.

"Cool," Asher said. "Look, I've got to get to my class. See you around, okay?"

"Sure," Arielle said, waggling her fingers. "Bye."

I rolled my eyes. "Now who's obvious?" I said.

"Totally," Traci agreed.

Arielle just smiled and stayed rooted to the spot, staring after Asher as he hurried off down the hall. "He is *really* cute," she said.

"Hey, I've got a good idea, Arielle," I said. "Why don't *you* run for sixth-grade class president?"

Arielle shrugged. "Nah. Too boring."

"But it's okay for *me?*" I asked.

"Well, yeah," Arielle said. "I mean, you're so good

at that kind of stuff. Talking about things you think are important and then taking action."

I hated to admit it, but Arielle had a point. I love to talk about issues that are important to me and then make a difference. I just wasn't sure I had what it takes to lead my whole sixth-grade class.

Or did I?

chapter
THREE

Note on the McClintic family fridge

Kids—
Don't even <u>think</u> about making a snack unless you're planning to clean up your mess! Please be considerate of other family members.

Love, Mom

P.S. Dave, use a <u>glass</u> for the OJ!

"Hey, pass the popcorn, guys," Arielle said. "You're hogging it."

I grinned and pretended to cover the big blue bowl in front of me on the McClintics' kitchen table. "What's the magic word?"

"Please, please, *pleeeeease*," Felicia said, reaching over and helping herself to the last few kernels of popcorn.

Traci shook her head. "That's the second bowl already. Guess we'll have to make some more."

"What else do you have?" Arielle asked. "Any cookies?"

"Popcorn's a lot healthier," I pointed out. "Except when you pour all that butter on it, like the last batch."

"Let's have both, then," Arielle said as Traci dumped a giant box of Oreos in front of her.

"Just what I was thinking," Felicia said with a grin.

Traci went over to the cupboards and pulled out another bag of microwave popcorn. "So Amanda, have you decided yet if you're going to run for class president?"

"Well, I'm thinking about it," I said. "I just feel like I need some time to think about what my platform would be. And whether I'd make a good leader."

Arielle twisted apart a cookie and scraped off a piece of vanilla creme with her finger. "Well, you really don't have much time to waste," she said. "The debate is only a week away."

"We can help you with your speech and put up a whole bunch of posters at school," Felicia offered.

"And get all those kids to sign your petition," Arielle added.

"You'll need a campaign slogan, too," Traci said, bringing over the fresh popcorn. "How about 'Be Cool, Vote Kepner'?"

"Sounds like a soda ad," Arielle said.

Traci put her hands on her hips. "Can *you* come up with anything better?" she asked.

Just then Traci's brother, Dave, came into the

kitchen, carrying his skateboard. He was dressed in some baggy pants and a T-shirt that said SK8 FOR LIFE. He looked really cute. Feeling my cheeks start to blush, I concentrated on the cookies.

"Anything better than what?" he asked.

"None of your business," Traci said quickly, pushing him toward the door. "Heading to the skate park?"

Dave walked over and grabbed a handful of fresh popcorn. "Looks like it, huh, Trace-Face?" he said. "Me and Mac almost have our 360s nailed."

"Wow, that's pretty impressive," I spoke up. "You guys must be good."

Dave flushed. "We're okay." He reached for more popcorn.

"Make your own," Traci told him, taking the bowl away. "We're having a private party here. No brothers allowed."

I could never get why Traci was always trying to send Dave away. It wasn't like he was doing anything wrong. Maybe it was just that I didn't have any brothers or sisters around my age. "We're celebrating being un-grounded," I told him.

"And convincing Amanda to run for class president," Arielle added.

Dave leaned against the kitchen counter. "Yeah? I think you'd be great, Amanda."

I smiled, hoping he couldn't tell how my stomach just flipped over.

"That's what everyone says," Felicia told him.

This whole thing was getting embarrassing now. "Well, thanks, guys," I said. "But—"

"She's definitely going to do it," Arielle said. "Aren't you, Amanda?"

I looked down at the table. I could feel my friends—and Dave—staring at me. But the truth was, I still couldn't make up my mind. It was one thing to join student government, to be part of a whole group of kids. But actually being in charge of things . . . that was a totally different deal. And a lot of hard work.

"Well, I'd go for it if I were you, Amanda," Dave said. "You're so . . . um . . . smart." His voice suddenly cracked.

Arielle giggled.

"Shhh!" Felicia whispered.

I stole a glance sideways at Dave. He looked so uncomfortable, I felt really bad. I knew he was just trying to be nice. That's what I liked best about him. He was so sweet for a guy, even if Traci didn't agree. And I had a feeling maybe Dave liked me back. But then, he was Traci's *brother*, for heaven's sake. Awkward city.

It was definitely time to switch subjects.

"So, what's the deal with Healing Paws?" I asked my friends, looking around the table. "Are we still going to the hospital this weekend?"

"I guess we can, since we're not grounded anymore," Felicia said. "Thank goodness."

"Well, count me in," Traci said. "I can't wait to see the animals again."

Healing Paws is a program that's really important to us. Felicia's dad runs the Wonder Lake Animal Shelter just outside of town, and the four of us help him out there a lot. We all love animals. Well, Arielle *sort of* likes them. Anyway, we had this idea to take some of the animals to visit kids who were sick in the hospital. The kids love it and so do the animals. Plus it's a great way to get publicity for the shelter. Mr. Fiol needs donations to keep it running. And sometimes people who hear about Healing Paws decide to adopt a great pet.

"Maybe we should visit the hospital the Saturday after instead," Arielle said. "That way we could do something really fun this weekend to celebrate being un-grounded."

"*What!?*" Traci practically jumped out of her chair. "How can you *say* that, Arielle? Being with the animals is *tons* of fun."

"I didn't say it wasn't fun," Arielle said. "But you and I have a soccer game this Saturday morning, remember? And we need to get started on Amanda's campaign, too."

"Hey, wait a minute," I began. "I haven't decided—" But then I gave up. No one was really listening. They were too busy arguing.

"Besides, the kids are counting on us," Traci was saying.

"And so is my dad," Felicia put in.

Arielle held up her hands. "Okay, okay. Sorry. It was just an idea. Count me in, too."

Traci sat back down again.

"Well, that's settled," I said with a sigh. "So Felicia, what's been going on at the shelter lately? Any news?"

"Any new animals?" Traci asked eagerly. She's a huge dog lover, but she can't have one because Dave is allergic.

"I'm not really sure," Felicia replied. "I've been mostly at my mom's for the last week. But I did hear that Angel and Snowflake got adopted by a really nice family with two little girls."

"That's great," I said, nodding. Angel and Snowflake are the cutest kittens you ever saw. They're both these fuzzy white fur balls, and they look exactly alike. Except Angel has a smudge of black on her nose. And Snowflake has one blue eye and one green one.

"Penny was supposed to go to the hospital with us on Saturday," Felicia said. "But she may not be able to now. Something about a sculpture she has to finish for a big art show coming up."

"Oh," I said. "It must be really important, then." I couldn't help feeling a little sad. How come Felicia knew what Penny was doing lately and I didn't? Penny was *my* baby-sitter. I mean, my friend. Way before she became Felicia's dad's girlfriend. But I hadn't seen her

30

much lately, and now Felicia seemed to know more about Penny than I did.

"But I'm not really sure about that," Felicia said quickly, seeing the expression on my face. She must have realized that I was feeling a little left out. "Penny mostly hangs out with my dad."

I threw Felicia a grateful look. "Right," I said. "Well, that's okay. The four of us and your dad can handle the animals ourselves."

"Do you have any soda?" Arielle asked Traci. "These cookies are making me really thirsty."

"We have orange juice," Traci said. "And milk and Gatorade."

"I'm allergic to milk," Arielle said.

Dave suddenly cleared his throat. "Um, I could help you guys on Saturday if you want. At the hospital."

We all turned to stare at him. Traci's mouth dropped open.

"Dave, that's really nice of you," I said. "But you're allergic to every animal on earth!"

Dave shrugged. Was it just me, or was *he* blushing now? "I'll be okay."

Traci frowned. "We can't have you sneezing all over the kids."

"Maybe we could take some of the kids and the animals outside this time," I suggested.

"And bring lots of tissues," Felicia added.

31

"I don't get it, Dave," Traci said, frowning. "Why do you want to go so much?"

"I think *I* know," Arielle said. She glanced at me and snickered. I tried to discreetly kick her under the table with my purple clogs.

"It's no big deal, Trace-Face," Dave said, taking a juice box from the fridge. "I'm just not that busy on Saturday."

"Well, we *could* use the extra help," Arielle pointed out. "Some of the animals get a little crazy when they get excited."

"They do not," Traci told her.

"Okay, okay," I said, holding up my hands. Arielle and Traci were always arguing. Arielle and I bickered sometimes, too. But that was different—we knew each other so well, we were like an old married couple. Traci and Arielle were just so different that they clashed a lot. "Saturday, all five of us, meet at the shelter at noon. Agreed?"

We all slapped hands.

"Well, I'm out of here," Dave said, picking up his skateboard from where he'd leaned it against a counter. "Mac's probably waiting for me."

"About time," Traci said under her breath.

"Bye," I said. Dave nodded and waved.

As soon as Dave had left the house, Arielle and Felicia started to giggle. "Someone's in *loooove*," Arielle teased.

"And he's even willing to risk sneezing to death," Felicia said. "That is *so* romantic."

I crossed my arms. "You two are nuts," I said. "I think all that sugar has affected your brains."

"Okay, Amanda Panda," Arielle said. "We won't bring up your boyfriend again."

"Even though you two are so obviously in love with each other," Felicia added, grinning.

"Guess we'll have to change the campaign slogan when Amanda and Dave get married," Arielle said. "'Be Cool. Vote McClintic.'"

"Hey, gross, you guys!" Traci broke in. "That's my *brother* you're talking about!"

Traci's face was kind of purple. I'm sure mine was, too, from total embarrassment. Friends can be such a pain sometimes.

It was time to get back to business, I thought. "Let's start making plans for Saturday," I said. I took out my day planner from my knapsack. "Felicia, which animals do you think your dad will want to bring this time?"

"You're no fun." Arielle pouted.

"Sorry," I said, flipping to October 2. "We have very important things to discuss here."

"I'd much rather discuss you and *Dave*," Arielle teased.

"Quit it, Arielle!" Traci warned. She reached for the popcorn bowl.

I concentrated on starting a list at the top of the page. "Animals to Bring on Saturday."

Arielle turned to Felicia. "Isn't Amanda amazing? She can totally concentrate on Healing Paws stuff, even when she has a big wedding to plan. That's why she'll make such a great class president. She's a multi-tasking genius."

"Okay, that's enough!" I said, clenching my teeth. I looked at Traci. "Ready?" I asked.

Traci nodded. "You bet," she said.

The two of us reached into the big blue bowl and took out huge handfuls of popcorn. Then we both started chucking kernels at Arielle and Felicia.

"Hey, watch it!" Arielle protested. "You'll get butter on my new shirt."

"It'll come out," I told her, throwing more popcorn. "Eventually."

Felicia shielded her face. "Ewww, gross! It's in my hair!"

In retaliation, Arielle crumbled a bunch of Oreos in her hands and threw them at me. But she missed and the crumbs fell all over the floor.

Traci stopped throwing popcorn for a minute. "Oh, wait a minute, guys," she said. "My mom's going to kill me if we make a mess."

"Too late," Felicia said gleefully. She reached to grab the popcorn bowl but missed and knocked over my glass.

Splat. Sticky orange juice everywhere.

Soon the four of us were going crazy, throwing everything we could find—popcorn, cookies, pretzels, M&M's. We were laughing and squealing and screaming at the top of our lungs.

The McClintics' kitchen had become a battle zone, but we couldn't stop.

Until Traci's mom walked in the door with a bagful of groceries. And she didn't look very happy.

Uh-oh.

Busted!

chapter
FOUR

Note stuck in Amanda's locker

Hi, Amanda,
    Your soccer friend told me you're definitely going to run for 6th-grade prez. All right!!
    See you later,

                              Asher

The next morning at school, I found a piece of notebook paper folded in the door of my locker. When I ripped it out and read it, I was *not* happy.

At all.

"I'm going to kill you, Arielle," I said. "For real this time."

Arielle leaned against the locker next to mine and smiled. "No, Amanda. You're going to *thank* me. I actually did you a huge favor. You'll be the best class president this school has ever seen."

I sighed. "You think so?" I asked. Arielle looked like the picture of self-confidence in her fuzzy red sweater, black velvet hair band, and black capri pants.

I wondered if I had the self-confidence to put myself in front of our whole class.

"Absolutely," Arielle said.

I took out the books I needed for the morning and shut my locker. Arielle was waving to some seventh-grade guy in the hall.

"I never totally made up my mind about running, you know," I said.

"Sure, you did," Arielle said. "You're just worried about taking the plunge, that's all. But it won't be so bad, really. I'm going to help you."

I hate it when my best friend is right. "I think you've helped enough," I said.

"Well, you can't back out now," Arielle said. "Asher is counting on you."

"I can't believe you actually talked to him already." I checked my watch. "It's only eight forty-five A.M. How did you manage that?"

Arielle smiled. "Easy," she said. "I called him as soon as I got home from Traci's yesterday."

"You're kidding," I said, feeling anger welling up inside me. "You mean you used this whole Amanda's-running-for-president thing as an excuse to call a cute boy?"

"Something like that," Arielle said, studying her fingernails. They were red today, to match her sweater. I couldn't believe she didn't even notice I was upset.

"Well, guess what? Now you have a chance to talk to Asher again. You can call him right back up and tell him

37

that you made a teensy, tiny mistake. Because I quit!"

"You can't quit," Arielle said calmly. "Not now."

"Watch me," I shot back.

"No, I mean you really *can't*." Arielle sounded serious.

I sighed as the two of us started walking toward homeroom. "Oh, really? Why not?"

Arielle gave me that angelic smile of hers that's so totally fake. "I signed you up."

I stopped right in the middle of the crowded hall. *"WHAT???"* I practically screamed. I swear, I was shaking so much that I almost dropped my books.

"Well, I thought I'd save you some time, since you'll have so much to do soon," Arielle explained. "I just happened to be going by the student government office this morning, so I picked up that petition. You know, the one you need fifty kids to sign?"

I braced myself. "Yeeeeees," I said, trying to stay calm. "Go on. Please."

"You're going to be so happy," Arielle said. "I went back and got fifty-TWO signatures from a bunch of kids hanging out on the lawn."

"Is that by any chance why you told me and Felicia that you had something really important to do this morning?" I asked. Traci's mom had driven her to school. Ms. McClintic was still really mad about the huge mess we'd made in the kitchen yesterday. It had taken forever for the four of us to clean it up.

"That's right," Arielle said. "Aren't you happy?"

I closed my eyes. "No," I said. "I'm not. I know you meant well, but I can't believe you did this without asking me."

"Oh, but it's going to be great!" Arielle said. She grinned. "Madam President."

Some guy I didn't even know clapped me on the shoulder as he passed by with his friends. "Hey, good luck, Miranda," he said.

"Amanda," I corrected him.

"Thanks, Carter!" Arielle called after him. "Good luck in the game Saturday."

"You're unbelievable," I told my best friend since pre-K through gritted teeth. "You really are."

"Look, there's McClintic," Arielle said brightly. "You'd better not be late after yesterday."

"Right," I said with a sigh, following her through the classroom door.

Dee Dee McKenzie, a cute, tiny girl with long brown curly hair, waved to me wildly from across the room as Arielle and I walked in.

"Amanda!" she called. "Come on over!"

I clasped my books to my chest and walked over to where Dee Dee was sitting with her best friend, Nicole George. "Hi, Dee Dee, Nicole," I said with a smile. "How's it going?" I didn't know either of them that well, actually. But they'd always seemed pretty nice. Dee Dee was the captain of the Sixth-Grade Spirit Squad. She'd been elected last week.

"Everything's just fine," Dee Dee said, smiling. She had the whitest, most perfectly straight teeth I'd ever seen. Nicole had braces, big blue eyes, and long blond hair that curled at the end. I'd never heard her actually say anything.

"Um, great," I said, feeling a little awkward. What was going on here? Dee Dee was still smiling at me.

"Listen, Amanda, I want you to know, there aren't any hard feelings on my end or anything," she said.

"I'm not sure what you mean," I said, frowning.

"Well, just because we're running against each other doesn't mean we can't be friends," Dee Dee went on. "May the best candidate win."

"*Oh*," I said as it all came together. So Dee Dee was running for sixth-grade class president, too. She was pretty popular, though she didn't know as many kids as Arielle. Could I possibly beat her? I had no idea. Then I reminded myself: Popularity wasn't important. The issues were. I shouldn't even be thinking stuff like that.

"No problem, Dee Dee," I said. "I'll look forward to the debate. Hey, who knows, it may even be fun!"

I just hope that's true, I thought.

When I walked over to my seat, Arielle was smiling. "You can beat Dee Dee, no sweat," she said. "She's not very aggressive. And I bet she doesn't even have her petition signed yet. I made sure I got to everyone before she did this morning."

"Hey, Amanda," Traci greeted me. "Arielle just told me the good news about your running. Congrats."

"Gee, thanks," I said, throwing a sideways glare at Arielle. "I think the whole school's heard by now."

"I hope so!" Arielle said. "That's good PR."

"You know," I told her in a low voice, "just because kids signed my petition doesn't mean they'll all vote for me. It just means I can put my name on the ballot."

"Who cares?" Arielle said, shrugging. "At least I got your name out there. That means I'm a good campaign manager."

"Well, yeah," I said, smiling in spite of myself. "You sure are."

The truth was, Arielle was right. This time. I realized now that I really *did* want to run for sixth-grade class president. I'm usually gutsier about making decisions and acting on them. But this whole class election thing was different somehow. More personal, I guess. I'd be putting me, Amanda Kepner, on the line. And that was kind of scary.

Besides, I *hated* to lose. Almost as much as Arielle when she wanted something—or when she and Traci were out on the soccer field.

But I always kept that little factoid about myself private. Maybe it wouldn't be private for long.

Arielle met me outside my last-period gym class. "Your hair's all wet," she said, squinting at me. "Why did you take a shower if you're going home now?"

"I have to baby-sit Jessy and Joey until Penny gets there," I said. "Mrs. Delson leaves at three today. And you know how the twins are. I'd never get a minute to myself."

"Oh," Arielle said. "Rats. I thought maybe we could go to the Sweet Shoppe. Well, listen, I'm coming home with you, then."

"I'm not sure that's such a good idea," I said. "Remember what happened last time you helped me baby-sit?" Arielle had actually locked Jessy and Joey in the den by mistake.

"I'm not going to baby-sit," Arielle said. "I'm going to help you with your campaign stuff. We've got to get started right away. Felicia and Traci have orchestra practice, so it'll just be you and me."

"Well, okay," I said slowly. "But I'll have to keep an eye on the twins at the same time. I guess we can start listing some ideas for the debate, though."

Arielle waved a hand. "That's way down the road, Amanda," she said. "What you want to do first is get a bunch of posters up."

"You think so?" I said doubtfully. "Well, okay. But I'm not sure if I have any poster board. I could ask my dad to take me to the mall when he gets home, but he'll probably be really tired. He's been working a lot lately and—"

"No problem," Arielle broke in. "I already went to the art room and got a bunch of supplies."

"You did?" I said. "You mean, they just gave stuff to you?"

"Sure," Arielle said. "It's for a school project, right? Sort of. Ms. Kinsella told me I could take what I wanted."

I shook my head. When Arielle puts her mind to something, she's practically unstoppable. Her mind is always clicking. I'm more the slow and steady type, I guess.

We almost missed the bus because we had to stop by Arielle's locker to get all the art supplies. There was a ton of it—poster board, colored pencils, paint, glue, colored tissue, scissors—and glittery markers.

"Um, Arielle, don't you think maybe this is all a bit much?" I asked. "I was planning something a little more . . . simple and to the point. I'm not really into glitter."

"This will get people's attention," Arielle said. "You need to make a statement."

"Whatever," I said. It wasn't worth arguing over. I knew I needed to save all my energy to deal with Jessy and Joey for the rest of the afternoon.

As soon as Arielle and I reached the steps to my house, twin redheads popped up at the living room window. "She's here, she's here!" we heard through the glass. "Mandy, Mandy, Mandy! And Awee-elle!"

"Uh-oh," I said to Arielle. "They sound even more wired than usual."

"They're really cute when they're quiet," Arielle said.

"Mmmm," I replied. I had a bad feeling about this.

Sure enough, Mrs. Delson looked exhausted when she came to the door. She was already pulling on her coat. "Hello, Amanda, Arielle," she said. "Sorry, but I'm in a huge hurry today. The children both had naps after school, so they're well rested. But if you want my advice, I wouldn't give either of them any sugar. It makes them a little . . . wild."

"Thanks, Mrs. Delson," I said.

"Let's get started on the posters right away," Arielle said as we headed inside.

"Maybe we should make sure the kids are settled first," I told her.

Jessy and Joey were waiting for us expectantly at the kitchen table. "Crayons!" Joey cried. "Cardboard!"

"You're going to make us a dollhouse!" Jessy shouted.

"No! A garage for my cars," Joey corrected.

"Sorry, guys," I told them. "Arielle and I have to make some signs for school."

"No!" Joey said.

"No!" Jessy echoed.

Things didn't get much better from there. I tried everything—videos, music, Barbies, Hot Wheels, even my hamster, Scurry, to keep the twins busy, but nothing held their attention for long. They wanted to be with me and Arielle in the kitchen.

"Okay, Jessy," Arielle said finally, putting down her hot-pink marker. "I'll make you a deal. If I French-braid your hair, will you go in the den and watch TV?"

Jessy brightened. "Okay," she said.

"Where's Joey?" I asked Arielle, frowning.

"Oh, he's in the den, watching a superhero video," she answered breezily. "It lasts a whole hour. I gave him some cherry soda and cookies, too. That made him really happy."

I put my head in my hands. "S-soda?" I repeated in horror. "Cookies?"

"No fair!" Jessy cried. "I want cookies, too!"

"Oops," said Arielle. "I forgot. They're not supposed to have sugar, huh?"

I raced into the den. There were cookie crumbs all over the couch and an empty drink cup. But no Joey.

I finally found him in the bathroom, stuffing an entire roll of toilet paper down the toilet.

By the time I finally corralled both the twins, calmed them down, and got them busy decorating their own little squares of cardboard, it was almost five o'clock.

"So, what do you think?" Arielle asked me, holding up the poster she'd been working on.

It said: VOTE FOR AMANDA "SPECIAL" K. TODAY!

"I dunno, Arielle," I said. "I sound like . . . some kind of cereal. It has nothing to do with what kind of candidate I am."

Arielle frowned. "What are you talking about?" she

said. "Who cares what it says? It's a nice, catchy slogan. And anyway, it's bright. Look, I put red, white, and blue sparkles all over the background. That makes the whole thing look really patriotic. You know, for the political theme."

"Right," I said, sighing. "That's great. Thanks." There was no use arguing with my friend. After all, it *was* nice of her to help me like this. But . . .

"What's the matter?" Arielle asked.

"Nothing," I said quickly. "Really."

Arielle put down her poster. "Come on, Amanda. Spill it."

I took a deep breath. This wasn't going to be easy. But maybe I should just tell the truth.

"Well, um . . . I kind of think . . . we should go with a more straightforward approach," I said finally. "About the issues. Sort of no-frills."

"I don't get it," Arielle said, eyeing her poster again. "You don't like the sparkles?"

"No, they look great," I lied. "They're just not my style, that's all. I guess I'm more interested in working on my campaign platform than the PR. I mean, ideas are the whole point of running, right?"

"Amanda, you're hopeless," Arielle said. "You'll never get elected with that kind of attitude."

Just then Penny burst into the kitchen. She has her own key to our house, but she scared us, anyway. And she had this weird look on her face.

"Amanda! And Arielle! Thank goodness!" she cried. "I was so worried."

"Worried?" I said. "Why?"

"Felicia and Traci have been trying to call you," Penny said, leaning against the refrigerator and breathing hard. "There's something wrong with the phone line."

Arielle and I both turned to look at the phone on the wall. The receiver was dangling from its cord, beeping.

"Uh-oh," I said. "The twins. Guess we didn't notice."

Penny threw up her hands. "Arielle, what about your cell phone?"

Arielle checked her backpack. "Battery's dead. Sorry."

"I almost called the police," Penny said. "The girls were expecting you at the animal shelter hours ago. But I knew you were going to be with Jessy and Joey until I got here, so . . ."

"The shelter?" I said.

"Oh, noooo," Arielle said, suddenly clapping a hand to her mouth. "I totally messed up."

"Messed up *how?*" I asked suspiciously. "Help me out here."

"I guess I got things a little confused," Arielle told me. "I thought Felicia and Traci had orchestra practice this afternoon. But maybe that's tomorrow. I just remembered, they said something at lunch about meeting at the shelter and I said I'd tell you. Then I forgot."

I just stared at my friend in disbelief.

Penny walked over and replaced the receiver on the hook. She didn't say anything, either. What was the point?

"Why were we supposed to go to the shelter?" I asked finally. "Is anything wrong? We're still going to the hospital for Healing Paws tomorrow, right?"

"I think the girls said something about getting the dogs ready," Penny told us.

Just then the phone rang. Maybe we should have left it off the hook.

"I can't believe you blew us off!" Traci said immediately. "Thanks a lot, Amanda! Arielle's with you, isn't she? What were you guys doing that was so *important?*"

As Traci was yelling at me, our call-waiting beeped. "Hold on just a second," I told her. "I'm really sorry. It may be my dad or stepmom."

Nope. It was Asher Bank.

I almost dropped the phone. How had he gotten my number? *Easy enough*, I told myself. How many Kepners were there in Wonder Lake? But I had to get back to Traci. Fast. She'd sounded really mad.

"Hi, Asher," I said. "Listen, I'll have to call you back, okay? Can you give me your number?"

I wrote it down on the memo board next to the phone. Then I went back to Traci. "Look, I'll just see you at noon tomorrow," she said. She sounded completely exasperated. "Don't forget this time, okay?"

Then the phone clicked in my ear. I stood there

48

holding it for a minute, too startled to react. Traci didn't even give me a chance to explain! She should know me better than to think I would blow off the animal shelter. I loved animals as much as her!

I clunked the receiver back into its cradle, maybe a little harder than necessary. Sometimes I just couldn't win.

chapter
FIVE

PrincessA: Hey, it's me again! Whatcha doing?
FlowerGrl: TRYING TO GET SOME WORK DONE!
PrincessA: Oh. What r u doing?
FlowerGrl: CAN'T TALK NOW. SORRY! :-(

That night I stayed up really late, working on my campaign platform. I came up with a lot of ideas to help improve our school. Sure, students didn't have the power to change things all by themselves. But the administration listened to what we have to say. Our opinions counted.

Of course, preserving the WLMS arts budget was the biggest part of my platform. I had to tell the students what was really going to happen and explain to them how arts and sports were equally important to our school. I knew that once I gave my classmates the facts, they would see themselves that the arts program had to stay.

Besides that, I had some great ideas for programs

and events. I already had some experience with fund-raising. Like the party we had for the animal shelter about a month ago. And I knew we could get a whole bunch of parents and kids and people from the town to pitch in and give the school a new coat of paint. I also thought it would be great if students got to know their teachers better. Maybe we could have an assembly once a month where the teachers could tell us about themselves. And what about a "buddy" system at the beginning of the school year for sixth graders and eighth graders? Arielle would love that. *Especially* if she got paired with Asher Bank.

The weird thing was, now that I was really thinking about the things that were important to me, I was realizing just *how* important they were. And I was thinking about how great WLMS could be if I could just put my plans into action. And I think that's when competitive Amanda sat up and took notice. I wasn't just running because I had to anymore. Now that I started planning, I really *wanted* to win.

There was a knock on my bedroom door. "Amanda?" my dad called. "Are you still awake, honey?"

"Yep," I said. "Come in."

My dad peeked his head through the door. He was still wearing his shirt and tie from work. "I saw your light on," he said. "You really need to get some sleep."

"So do you," I told him.

It was true. My dad looked terrible. He's been

working late at the office every night for weeks. It probably didn't help that Jessy and Joey were still bouncing off the walls. I could hear them in their room right now, singing TV jingles again and again. Even Penny hadn't been able to calm them down. Cherry soda must be supersugary. I made a mental note to tell my stepmom never to buy it again.

Dad just nodded tiredly. "Well, good night, sweetheart. It's after ten. Shut down your computer now, okay?"

"Sure, Dad," I said. "I'm almost done."

Actually, I was glad it was so late. At least the phone had stopped ringing off the hook. Arielle had been calling me practically nonstop all night. She wanted to fill me in on what Felicia had said and what Traci had said. Traci was still mad about our blowing them off by mistake this afternoon. At least Felicia was coming around. It still bothered me that Traci was being so bullheaded in thinking I had ignored them on purpose. It seemed like there wasn't anything I could do or say to make it any better.

All I could do was hope everything would be okay by tomorrow.

Maybe I should look up some old presidential campaign speeches, I thought, clicking on my Internet connection. Running for president of the United States wasn't quite the same as running for sixth-grade class president. But maybe it would help me get in the spirit of things.

I checked my E-mail one more time. To my surprise, there was a note from Dee Dee McKenzie.

```
Hi, Amanda,
    Just wanted to tell you again that I'm glad
it's YOU running against me. Good luck and
may the best candidate win!
    P.S. Did you do the English essay?
```

I frowned. Dee Dee seemed really nice. But why was she glad she was running against *me?* Did she think I'd be easy to beat?

Quit thinking like that, I told myself. *Positive attitude!* You *have the ideas. She just doesn't know what a fierce competitor you really are!*

I was about to reply to Dee Dee when an IM suddenly popped up on my computer screen. Arielle, of course. Again.

```
PrincessA: Hey! Can u call me?
```

I sighed. I really didn't want to talk about who said this about what and how mad Traci and Felicia still were at us. I had better things to do. I typed my answer.

53

FlowerGrl: Can't. It's after 10. Kepner family rules, remember? What's wrong?

PrincessA: Have to ask u something. It's Friday nite. Your parents won't mind. Mine don't.

Okay, that's it, I thought. I was beginning to feel really annoyed. Arielle had been bugging me all night. I couldn't concentrate. I needed to tell her to stop, because my hints weren't working.

In one swift motion I disconnected the phone line from my computer. Then I plugged it back into the phone on my nightstand.

Almost immediately it rang.

Now you're toast, PrincessA, I thought. Luckily I caught it on the first ring, so my dad didn't hear.

"Hello?" I said in a not-very-nice tone.

"Amanda?" the person on the other end asked. But it wasn't Arielle. It was a guy.

Yikes! I never called Asher back! How could I have forgotten? For some reason, Arielle hadn't mentioned it all night. Now I actually wished she had.

"Amanda, this is Asher again. I'm really, really sorry to call so late," he said. "Did I wake anyone up?"

"No," I said, listening to the twins jumping on their mattresses. "Not at all."

"Listen, I was wondering whether you need help with any of your campaign stuff," he said. "I know there isn't a lot of time to prepare for the debate. Maybe I could give you a few pointers."

"Really?" I said. My mind was spinning. This was awesome! With my ideas and Asher's political expertise, I could be almost unbeatable! "Well, gosh . . . thanks," I told him. "I've been working a lot on some ideas. But to tell you the truth, I've never spoken in front of people. In fact, I'm kind of freaked out about it."

Asher laughed. "No big deal," he said. "I used to get really nervous all the time, but I've gotten much better. My girlfriend helped me."

Girlfriend? Aha! So I was right—Asher definitely didn't like me! Arielle had been totally wrong about him not dating anyone. Maybe she went to a different school or something.

"I've got a family birthday party to go to on Sunday," Asher went on. "But maybe we could get together tomorrow for an hour or two."

Tomorrow? I frowned. Tomorrow my friends and I were going to the hospital for Healing Paws.

"Ummm . . ."

A million thoughts started flying through my head. Like about all the issues I had been putting together for my platform, and how important they were to me, and how much I needed to get elected to put those ideas in motion. My friends would *kill* me if they knew I was blowing off Healing Paws to work on my campaign. But then, it wasn't like they had been completely fair to me today. Traci and Felicia wouldn't even listen to my side of the story. And Arielle—well, Arielle had started all the trouble in the first place. And she hadn't been very apologetic about it.

"How about if we meet in the morning?" Asher was saying. "Like at eleven-thirty. We could work for a while, then grab a pie at Wonder Lake Pizza or something."

I hesitated. I was supposed to meet my friends for Healing Paws at noon. But eleven-thirty was pretty early . . . maybe I could be a little late for Healing Paws. I could meet everybody at the hospital instead of at the shelter. I'd just tell them some kind of minor emergency had come up.

That was true, wasn't it? Arielle and Traci and Felicia would understand.

After all, Asher was a really busy guy. He had plenty of other things to do, I was sure. I should take this opportunity to get his advice while I could. And once I was class president—*if* I got elected, I reminded myself—I would spend all kinds of time with my friends helping the animals! Maybe I could even get some kind of program going at school.

"Okay," I told Asher. "That'd be great. And really, thanks. It's so, so nice of you to help me."

"It's a date, then," Asher said. "Wonder Lake Pizza. Eleven-thirty."

I frowned. Date? He was just kidding, right?

But Asher had already hung up.

I stared at the receiver in my hand for a minute. I had a funny feeling in my stomach, like I had just done something that I would regret. *But why?* I asked myself. I had gone to Healing Paws faithfully ever since it started. Nobody loved animals more than me. And my friends . . . well, they would understand if they knew.

I put the receiver very carefully back on the hook.

The truth was, I *really* wanted to win the election now. I knew I was the best candidate for the job. And with Asher's help, I had a real shot. Was one teeny little white lie to my friends going to hurt so much?

No. Of course not.

I changed into my pj's and went down the hall to the bathroom. Miracle of miracles, the twins were finally quiet. I brushed my teeth, headed back to my bedroom, and hit the sack. I was going to have to call my friends tomorrow.

But no matter how hard I tried, I just couldn't get to sleep. I lay awake until almost midnight, staring at my purple lava lamp.

I wasn't feeling guilty, though.

Really.

Not at all.

chapter
SIX

Penny finally agreed to drop me off at Wonder Lake Pizza the next morning. But I could tell she wasn't very happy about it.

"Amanda, I think you're making a big mistake," she said as we drove toward the village green. Penny was on her way to meet Mr. Fiol and my friends at the animal shelter. She'd changed her whole schedule for the day so she could help us with Healing Paws. It was part of our plan to have Penny hang around with some of the animals, in the hope that she'd eventually get over her fear

58

of dogs. Now she was going to have to go without me.

I felt like a jerk.

"It'll be okay, Penny," I said hopefully. "I'll just be a little late, that's all. I'll call you when I'm ready to be picked up, and I'll meet those guys at the hospital, right?"

Penny sighed. "Okay, Amanda," she said. "But I'm not going to lie for you."

"I know," I said in a small voice. "I understand." I wasn't happy about the lying part, either. I had called Arielle and told her that I had to watch the twins for a while. I promised to catch up with her and the others later, if I could. Hopefully they wouldn't be too mad.

Ha. Fat chance. Especially after yesterday. Traci was probably still mad at me for that. And I wasn't sure about Felicia.

Arielle would get over it, of course. But what about Dave? He was going to be there today—and what if it *was* just because of me?

I shuddered, looking out the window. I couldn't feel much worse.

Arielle had seemed a little disappointed on the phone. Luckily she hadn't asked many questions. Family stuff wasn't that exciting. But if Arielle had known I was meeting Asher Bank for pizza—even for a totally nonromantic reason—she would have been all over me like sticky rice. I felt terrible keeping a secret from her.

As we pulled up to the pizza parlor, Penny stopped the car and looked over at me. "Are you sure winning this election is this important to you?" she asked. "More important than a promise you made to your friends?"

"Yes," I answered. "I mean . . . no. I don't know."

I saw Asher park his bike and head into the pizza parlor. He was carrying a notebook, and he looked really cute in his plaid shirt and WLMS baseball cap.

Why was I even thinking that? *This isn't a date*, I reminded myself. At least I didn't think so. It was business.

"I'd better go," I told Penny with a sigh.

"Okay, sweetie," she said with a frown. "See you later."

The chimes above the door sounded even louder than usual when I walked into Wonder Lake Pizza a few minutes later. The place was completely empty except for Asher. He was already sitting at a table.

"Amanda, hey!" he said. "Right on time."

I checked the big retro clock on the wall behind the counter. Eleven-thirty on the dot. That meant we had ninety minutes until Penny came back. Plenty of time to work.

Sal, the owner, came up to take our orders. "Well, hello there, Amanda," he greeted me. "Where are your friends today?"

I carefully studied the menu, even though I always have the same thing. One veggie special slice. "They're, um . . . busy, I guess," I said.

"Ah," Sal said. He winked at Asher. "She's a great

young lady," he said. "A little serious, maybe. But very nice."

My face was burning. I stared at the menu even harder. Obviously Sal thought Asher and I were on a date!

"Yeah," Asher said, smiling. "She reminds me of my cousin Hannah, actually."

Cousin? Gee, thanks, I thought. But at least it wasn't romantic. I still wasn't sure what Asher was hanging out with me for.

"I'll have two slices, I guess," Asher said. "One sausage and mushroom and one pepperoni, please."

"You got it," Sal told him. "How about you, Amanda? The usual?"

"Yes, please," I answered. I quickly handed him back the menu. For some reason I felt like Sal could read my mind. Did he know I had ditched my friends so I could hang out with Asher?

No, I told myself firmly. That was impossible.

"Let's get to work, okay?" Asher said. "We've got a lot to talk about."

That sounded like a fine idea to me. I sure didn't feel like trying to make conversation right now. I felt too . . . guilty.

After a few minutes, though, I began to relax a bit. Asher was easy to talk to.

"Forget about imagining your audience in their underwear when you're making a speech," Asher told me. "That never works."

"Really?" I asked. I had read that advice in a book once. "Why not?"

Asher grinned. "Well, for one thing, you might start cracking up," he said.

"True," I said, chuckling.

"It helps me to focus on a spot in the middle of the room. Or a friendly-looking person," Asher went on.

I asked Asher lots of questions. He showed me drafts of his old speeches and debate notes, just to give me some general ideas. We put our notebooks away when the pizza arrived so they wouldn't get greasy.

"So how's your friend Arielle?" Asher asked me, taking a bite of pepperoni. "You guys hang out together a lot, don't you?"

"Yeah," I said, nodding. "In fact, I'm supposed to—I mean, we've been best friends forever." I made a mental note to tell Arielle that Asher had asked about her. Then I remembered I couldn't.

Then suddenly I thought of something terrible. What if Asher happened to mention to Arielle that we'd seen each other over the weekend? Then she'd know I lied to her and Traci and Felicia.

That could happen! I thought wildly.

No, it can't, I corrected myself. I was getting totally paranoid now.

I tried to get back to business. "So should I try to add some jokes?" I asked. "Everyone seems to like funny speeches."

Asher shrugged. "I dunno. If you're comfortable using a lot of humor, sure. But it's hard to pull off. You might be better off sticking with a straightforward approach."

"That's what I told Arielle," I agreed. "I'm not sure I'm very funny."

"Well, I don't know about that," Asher said. "But I think you should just try to be yourself." He leaned forward across the table. "You want to hear something really funny?"

"Sure," I said.

"After I got elected class president and president of the student council, I had to make an acceptance speech," Asher began. "Sort of a thanks-for-voting-for-me-and-here's-what-we're-going-to-get-done-this-year deal."

I nodded.

"Everything went great until I finished the speech and started walking away from the podium," he went on. "Then I tripped on some wires and fell flat on my face."

I giggled. "Really?" I said. "You're kidding."

Asher shook his head. "I wish I was! It was like something out of a Jim Carrey movie. My friends still laugh about it."

I smiled. I was beginning to feel a little more confident. If Asher could get over being nervous and even messing up big time, then so could I.

We talked some more. Asher was full of funny stories but also really good advice. I wanted to soak up everything he said and use it in all of my campaign stuff. I told him some of my ideas, and he even gave me some great pointers for presenting them to my classmates and actually pulling them off. "That's the hard thing," he told me, "actually *doing* it once you've been elected." We both finished our pizza and I took pages and pages of notes. Finally I looked up at Sal's clock. And I was so shocked, I almost knocked over my soda.

It was almost three.

"Oh, my gosh," I blurted.

"What's wrong?" Asher asked.

"I, um—wow, it's really late." I started gathering up my notebooks and pens. "I should call my bab— uh, my friend Penny to come pick me up."

I looked up at Asher, expecting him to act surprised. But he wasn't even looking at me. His eyes were glued to the front of the store. "Hey, isn't that your friend Arielle?"

What?! I looked out the front windows, and sure enough, Asher was right—but it wasn't just Arielle! It was Arielle, Penny, Felicia, and Traci! And they were coming to Wonder Lake Pizza!

Oh *no*. This was a nightmare. I looked around, frantically searching for some means of escape. But there's only one door to Wonder Lake Pizza—the door my friends were walking through. My heart seemed to fall straight to my feet. What were they *doing* here? Healing Paws must be over! I was totally busted!

Luckily they didn't see me right away. Penny hurried into the pizza parlor right behind the girls. She glanced over at me, looking frantic and also apologetic. "I'm sorry," she mouthed silently to me.

I felt even worse when I saw who was behind Penny. Dave!

"What's the matter, Amanda?" Asher asked. "You look kind of weird. Is something wrong?"

"N-no," I stammered. "I'm fine." But my brain was clicking overtime. What should I do now? This was the worst moment of my entire life.

Just then Traci turned around and looked right at me and Asher. For a minute she didn't have any expression—it was like she just didn't believe what she was seeing. But then she looked completely shocked. It was almost as if the color was draining out of her face behind her freckles. In a few seconds she recovered and turned back around.

Grabbing Dave, she dragged him over to the specials board above the counter. "All of these sound kind of nasty to me," she said loudly. "Cheeseburger pizza, gross! Let's just have *real* burgers instead. We can go to Hamburger Heaven across the square."

"Hey, I like any kind of cheeseburger!" Dave protested. "Cheeseburger on pizza, cheeseburger at Hamburger Heaven, what's the difference?"

But Traci was already hustling her brother out the door. She didn't even glance back at me.

But Arielle and Felicia did. They must have seen

Traci's reaction when she looked over at me. They looked totally hurt when they saw me with Asher. And also, totally mad.

"Um, hamburgers sound good to me," Penny said brightly. "Let's go, ladies. My treat."

Sal was standing behind the counter. He kept opening and closing his mouth, but no words came out. He was literally speechless. I guess no one had called his pizza "nasty" before.

I couldn't believe it, either. Why had Penny brought my friends with her? What was she thinking?

But it wasn't Penny's fault, I knew. It was mine.

Asher shook his head. "That was the weirdest thing I ever heard," he said. "Why did they come in here if they didn't want pizza? And weren't those your friends?"

I looked down at the table. *They used to be*, I thought.

"Um, listen, Asher, I've got to go," I said, getting up from the table. "I have this emergency thing I just remembered I have to do. I really appreciate your helping me so much. And I had a great time, too. Thanks."

Then I threw down five dollars and two quarters on the table and ran out of Wonder Lake Pizza. I never wanted to step foot in there again.

My nondate with Asher Banks was *o-v-e-r*. So was my friendship with Arielle, Traci, and Felicia. And Dave. Whatever kind of relationship we had, I had just blown it big time.

How was I ever going to explain this whole mess?

chapter
SEVEN

E-mail from Amanda to the members of Healing Paws

To: PrincessA; sockrgrl0; FiFio1
From: FlowerGrl

    Guys, I know you're all really mad at me
because you're not answering my phone calls
even though I keep trying and trying and I'm
probably driving your families crazy. I am
so, SO sorry about what happened today. But
it isn't the way it looked, honest. PLEASE
let me explain!

After I left the pizza parlor, I went straight home.
That night Penny called and told me what had
happened. The girls and Dave had all wanted to
stop for a slice on the way back to the shelter in
Penny's car.

"I am *really* sorry, Amanda," Penny said. "I tried to
talk them out of it. But no go."

"That's okay," I said in a small voice. I didn't ask

her what they'd all said about me on the way to Felicia's. I didn't want to know.

All day Sunday, I tried to get in touch with my friends. I just *had* to apologize. I was sure they'd understand once I told them the whole story.

First I called Felicia, because she's always such a softie. But she wouldn't even come to the phone.

"I'm sorry, Amanda," her mom said. "Felicia's in the shower. And then she has a lot of homework to finish. I don't think she'll be able to call you back for a while."

Had Felicia told her mom she was mad at me? I couldn't tell, but I sure hoped not. It was so embarrassing. And I felt terrible about the whole thing.

It was just a misunderstanding, I told myself. A little white lie that backfired. As soon as my friends heard my explanation, everything would be fine between us. Right?

Next I tried Traci. She's usually pretty reasonable.

But not today.

"How could you blow us off *two* days in a row?" Traci practically exploded. "I thought you, of all people, Ms. Involvement and Commitment, cared about helping Healing Paws. And what about my poor brother? He was sneezing and choking all afternoon, hoping you'd show up at the hospital. He actually thinks you like him back."

"Traci, wait—" I began.

"Obviously he doesn't know what a liar and a sneak you really are," Traci rushed on. "Well, *I* do and . . ."

Suddenly I heard Dave's voice in the background. "Trace, have you seen my basketball?" I heard him say.

"No," Traci replied. "Go away."

"Hey, is that Amanda?" he asked. "Was everything okay with that big emergency yesterday? What *was* it, anyway?"

I cringed. But at least Dave didn't know the truth. Yet.

"Stop bugging me," Traci told him. "I've got to go," she told me.

Then she hung up.

Before I tried Arielle, I called Penny back for advice. "Help," I said, after I told her what had just happened.

"Sorry, sweetie," she said. "But you *did* lie to everybody. It always comes back to you in the end, like karma. Maybe you'll just have to let your friends cool off for a little while. You know, give them some space. Then you can try again. If that doesn't work, maybe I can talk to them."

"Thanks," I said, sighing. But as I hung up, I knew that I didn't want to let any more time pass. I had to make up with at least one friend. Right now.

I punched in Arielle's number. She was my oldest, bestest friend. I'd left her for last because I was sure she'd understand once she heard my explanation.

Besides, didn't Arielle know all about fudging the truth a bit sometimes? What was it she always said?

"Go after what you want, no matter what"? And hadn't Arielle been the one who'd wanted me to run for class president so badly in the first place?

She finally picked up the phone on about the tenth ring.

"What do *you* want, Amanda?"

Yikes, she sure sounded mad.

"Um, how did you know it was me?" I asked, stalling for time. How was I going to get Arielle to listen? I had the definite feeling from the sound of her voice that it wasn't going to be easy.

"Caller ID," Amanda answered. "But I figured you'd be calling me soon, anyway, trying to make up."

"Well, yeah," I said. "Look, Arielle, I know you're a little upset. But—"

"Upset? *UPSET?!*" Arielle's voice rose a few notches. I held the receiver out from my ear.

"You mean, just because you're obviously trying to steal Asher from me?" Arielle went on. "Well, forget it, Kepner. It's never going to work."

"What are you talking about?" I asked, frowning. Now I was getting mad myself. Arielle obviously wasn't going to listen.

"You know exactly what I'm saying," Arielle said.

And then it all clicked for me. Arielle thought I was on a *date* with *Asher*—the very same guy that she was seriously crushing on! It was such a mess, I didn't even know where to begin. Arielle knew me better than that!

"First of all, I thought you said Asher was crushing on *me*," I reminded her. "What do you mean, steal him from *you?*"

Arielle paused. "Well, maybe I was wrong about that," she said. "I've been talking with Asher a lot lately."

Sure, I thought. Here was a perfect example of Arielle fudging the truth.

"You're only interested in him because I am," she went on. "You are *so* competitive—and the sneakiest person I've ever met. Trust me, you'll be sorry."

Then Arielle hung up on me, just like Traci.

I was in shock. This was incredible. How could all three of my very best friends suddenly hate me?

I felt hot tears welling up in my eyes.

No class election could possibly be worth all this. Even if I won.

And I'd hardly even started my campaign yet!

chapter
EIGHT

Itemized bill from Quick-Os Copy Shop

10 Graphic design layouts, 5-color
30 Supersize copy enlargements
Specialty font
SUPER RUSH!!!!!
$110.00 paid in full
Credit card purchase

On Monday morning I was still totally miserable.

At breakfast my stepmom handed me a giant box of Special K. That made me think of the campaign slogan Arielle had made up for me. And then I felt worse.

"Amanda, what's wrong?" Adele asked. "You're sitting there at the table like a zombie. A very sad one."

I stared down into my empty bowl. I really didn't feel like talking about it. How could I tell Adele what a jerk I'd been on Saturday?

"Your dad told me you decided to run for class president after all." Now Adele was smiling. "You know, I was president of my class in high school. Every year. It was so much fun."

"That's great," I lied. I knew my stepmom meant well, but actually she wasn't helping. She was trying really hard to be perky.

The twins were sitting at the breakfast table, too. Sort of. Joey was building a tower of Cheerios, but he kept dropping most of them on the floor. Jessy jumped up about forty times to get more ice for her OJ from the automatic ice maker in the fridge. The machine made a really nasty grinding noise.

Adele put her hands to her temples. "Sit down, please, Jessy," she said. "No more ice."

My dad walked into the kitchen and went straight to the coffeemaker. "Hello, everyone," he said. "And good-bye. I'm late." He kissed each of us on the top of the head and headed out to the garage, mug and newspaper in hand.

I was really starting to worry about my dad. He'd been so totally stressed out lately. And Adele didn't seem much better. I wondered which was worse, dealing with crabby old Aunt Delores for a week or the twins 24/7? It was a close call.

There was no way I could tell either Dad or Adele about my problem with my friends. I'm sure they would have tried to help. But they already had plenty of other stuff on their minds.

I sat by myself on the school bus. For a while,

anyway. Then I started to feel silly. I'd have to start being a little more social if I wanted to get elected class president. I was going to have to make what Mr. Reid, my math teacher, calls an "effort."

Luckily none of my friends take the same school bus I do. Arielle used to live near me, but she went to private school back then. Now she lives way out by the river in a cool converted mill. Traci's house is in the other direction, and Felicia usually gets a ride to school with her dad. Or she takes the bus from town when she's staying at her mom's.

I got up from my seat and made my way to the back of the bus. "Hi," I told the two girls sitting in the last row. They looked like sixth graders. "My name's Amanda Kepner. I'm running for sixth-grade class president. I'd really appreciate it if you'd vote for me."

One of the girls smiled. "Sorry," she said. "But we're already voting for Dee Dee."

"Oh," I said. "Right. Um, the thing is—do you know about the arts budget?"

The girls looked at me like I was speaking Martian. "Arts budget?" one of them repeated. She looked at her friend and scrunched up her eyebrows. "I dunno, it sounds kind of boring."

"Boring?!" I could feel myself getting all worked up. This was exactly the kind of lack of interest that could cost us students a lot of arts money. "See, the school board wants to vote to take money away from arts and put it into the sports program."

"Oh," said the second girl. "That sounds like a good idea."

"It's not!" I said, and I could hear myself starting to sound upset. "See, if they take money away from arts, it means less art supplies, less music classes, less field trips to art museums. . . ."

The first girl looked at me and shrugged. "Sandy and I don't really care about that. See, we're on the Spirit Squad. We love sports."

"But don't you see—"

"Anyway, we're voting for Dee Dee," Sandy interrupted me. "So, um, good luck."

I looked at the two girls in surprise, then nodded. "Sure. Thanks," I said, backing away. "Um . . . think about what I said."

I went back to my seat, trying not to seem embarrassed. But also, I was feeling really frustrated. Those girls didn't care at all about a really important program that took place at their own school! If my whole class was like that, maybe I should stop trying to be social. I should just stick to my speeches and my debate preparations, and I'd really wow them in the end.

A guy I recognized from Spanish leaned across the aisle. He was wearing a WLMS football jacket.

"Hey, Kepner," he said. "If you get elected, you'll help get rid of that stupid arts program, right? Coach says it's draining money away from the team."

I just stared at him. How dumb could people be? Didn't they realize that the arts program was really important to WLMS?

"Um, I'll think about that," I told the football guy.

Politics was even tougher than I'd thought.

When I got off the bus, I headed straight to our usual before-school meeting spot on the front lawn, under the big maple tree. Maybe things would go better if I talked to my friends face-to-face.

Arielle and Traci were already there, but they were deep in conversation. It looked like they were talking about something really important.

But when they saw me coming, they both stopped talking.

Completely.

"Hi," I said, gulping. "How's it going?"

Neither of them answered.

I could tell that Traci felt kind of awkward. She kept switching the rolled-up poster she was holding from one hand to the other.

Arielle just stared straight through me.

That really bugged me. "Hello?" I said, waving my hand in front of her face. "Is anybody home?"

Arielle frowned and turned back to Traci. Arielle was carrying a rolled-up piece of cardboard, too. The two of them probably had a project due today or something.

"Come on, you guys," I pleaded. "Don't freeze me

out like this. You've got to listen to me. I was *not* on a date with Asher. And I didn't blow you guys off on purpose. I was going to come to the hospital, really. I just lost track of time."

Arielle and Traci exchanged glances. Then they both started walking toward the steps of the school.

"Asher was just helping me with my campaign," I said, hurrying after my ex-friends. "I swear."

Arielle looked back over her shoulder. "You're going to need help," she said. "A lot of it."

I stood there watching as Arielle and Traci blended into the crowd of noisy students filing into the building.

There wasn't anything else I could do.

Suddenly I had a terrible thought. What if those posters Arielle and Traci were carrying weren't for some class project? What if they were actually posters that said DON'T Vote for Amanda Kepner?

But it didn't matter, anyway. Because right then I made a decision.

I was dropping out of the race.

Being elected sixth-grade class president just wasn't worth losing my friends. And I was losing my enthusiasm for a big campaign, anyway.

Maybe if I quit, my friends would see that I was really sorry.

I'd go straight to the student government office and hand in my resignation from the race.

I headed slowly up the steps. Then I saw Felicia standing near the door, wearing a denim miniskirt and a bright yellow print blouse.

It seemed like she was looking for someone. And she was biting her pinky fingernail. She always does that when she's nervous.

We saw each other at the same time.

"Amanda," she greeted me in a flat tone. "Hi."

"Hi," I said.

For a second or two there was an awkward silence between us.

"You tried to call me yesterday," she said.

I looked down at the concrete. Then I took a deep breath. *Here goes nothing*, I thought. But what did I have to lose? My friends all hated me, anyway.

"I wanted to apologize," I said in a rush. "I really messed up."

Felicia didn't answer. I couldn't tell what she was thinking, either. But I told her the whole story.

At least she actually listened.

"Okay, Amanda," she said when I had finished. "I know you're sorry."

I nodded really hard.

"And I don't think Arielle and Traci will believe you."

My heart sank.

"But I do," Felicia said. "I was thinking about this whole thing a lot yesterday. I know you like Dave, not Asher."

For once I didn't even try to deny it. Okay, so I had a crush on Traci's brother. So what? At this point I had nothing to lose.

Except maybe my friends.

"I know you've always been totally into helping animals and just about every cause there is," Felicia went on. "And I also know you're not a very good liar." She smiled. "Neither am I."

I was actually beginning to feel a little better now. "So what should I do?" I asked Felicia as the two of us started walking into school together. "How can I make up with Arielle and Traci?"

Felicia bit her lip. "Well, maybe that's not such a good idea right now."

"What do you mean?" I asked.

She stopped in the middle of the lobby and shifted her knapsack to the other shoulder. "Um, well . . ."

"Felicia, guess what? I'm going to quit the campaign," I told her in a rush. "That way they'll see how totally sincere I am. I'm heading to the student government office right now to resign. I don't care about being class president. Not if it means that I'm going to lose my best friends."

Felicia put a hand on my arm. "Um, Amanda, there's something I should tell you," she said. "I think."

I frowned. That sounded serious. "What is it?" I asked. "Is it something bad?"

"Sort of," Felicia said. She sighed and looked away.

I followed the direction of her gaze. Then I almost had a heart attack.

Right above the WLMS trophy case against the wall was a huge, superflashy banner. It was hot pink with purple letters. And it said:

Vote Arielle Davis for 6th-Grade
Class President!!!

chapter
NINE

Announcement over WLMS PA system

Attention, WLMS students! There will a short, mandatory meeting for all class officer candidates today in the auditorium at two-thirty sharp. Please obtain a pass from your teacher to be excused early from your sixth-period class. This announcement is for class officer candidates ONLY! All other students will remain in their classes as usual.

I just stood there in shock in the middle of the school lobby. I couldn't stop staring at the ARIELLE DAVIS FOR PRESIDENT banner. Kids were pushing and shoving all around me, but I hardly even noticed.

"Um, Amanda?" Felicia asked, tapping me on the shoulder. "Maybe we should go."

"I can't believe it," I said, still dumbfounded.

Arielle, my oldest best friend—until yesterday—was actually going to run against ME?

"Is this some kind of joke?" I asked Felicia.

"Because if it is, it isn't funny. Is Arielle just trying to get back at me by putting up a fake sign?"

"I'm really sorry, Amanda," Felicia said softly. "But it's definitely real. Arielle said she was joining the race this morning."

"But the petition deadline is already past," I said, frowning.

Felicia shrugged. "I guess she's planning to run as a write-in candidate. Anyone can do that. And she does have a lot of friends, so . . ." Her voice trailed off.

"Well, let's get out of here," I said with a sigh. "We can't just stand here in the lobby forever." But the truth was, I couldn't stand seeing all the kids admiring Arielle's banner. It was definitely eye-catching. And also tacky.

Stop it, I scolded myself. *That's mean. And it's bad sportsmanship*, *too*. But that blaring pink-and-purple sign really bugged me. It practically screamed that Arielle Davis hated Amanda Kepner's guts. The whole thing might as well have been flashing in neon.

In fact, I was surprised Arielle didn't think of it.

Felicia and I headed down a side hall toward my homeroom. "I'll walk you," Felicia offered, even though her homeroom is in the other direction. I guess she felt sorry for me.

I was sure kids were whispering about me as we passed them. I saw one girl nudge another girl beside her and snicker.

"Looks like everyone's talking about you running for class president," Felicia said. "See, now you're famous at WLMS."

I knew Felicia was trying to make me feel better. But it wasn't working.

I felt even worse when the school secretary came over the PA system and announced a meeting for class officer candidates that afternoon.

"At least you get out of class," Felicia said. "Lucky you."

"All those kids are talking about Arielle running against me," I said, frowning. "Everyone knows we're really close friends. *Were*," I corrected myself quickly.

We walked the rest of the way in silence. All along the hall Arielle had put up fancy, professionally printed campaign posters. I couldn't bear to look at them. But everyone else was.

When we reached my homeroom, I didn't want to go in. I decided to wait until the very last minute. What was I going to say to Arielle and Traci now? What should I do?

One thing was for sure. I wasn't feeling so apologetic anymore about Saturday. Now I was just plain mad.

"You know, what you did on Saturday was rotten," Felicia said as I opened my locker. "You should have just told us the truth. But what Arielle is doing is pretty rotten, too."

I caught sight of myself in the little mirror on the

inside of my locker door. My eyes were brimming with tears. And I could practically feel my skin starting to break out from stress. I couldn't even answer Felicia. If I did, I might start crying.

"You'd make a much better president than Arielle," Felicia went on. "Because you really care. And you have great ideas. I bet you still win."

"It doesn't matter," I said. "I'm dropping out of the race. Arielle can be president if she wants. In fact, she can be queen. Or empress. Who cares?"

"Come on, Amanda," Felicia said. "You don't really mean that."

"Bet on it," I answered. But maybe it was true. I felt so hurt and angry and betrayed, I hardly knew what I was saying.

"Hey, what's in there?" Felicia asked. She pointed to the plastic bag I was trying to stuff into my locker.

"Nothing," I mumbled.

"No, really," Felicia said. "Are those your campaign posters?"

I looked down at the rolled-up pieces of cardboard poking out of the plastic bag. "Well, yeah," I said. "But I might as well throw them out now."

I'd made a whole bunch of posters on Saturday night, before I had decided for sure I was quitting.

"Wait a minute," Felicia said. "Let me see them."

I sighed and held out the bag. Felicia took it and

slowly unrolled one of the posters. "Wow," she said. "These are gorgeous."

"Thanks," I said.

I had worked really hard on them. Penny had even given me a few suggestions. They weren't attention grabbing like Arielle's fancy, printed ones. They were sort of quiet and low-key. And artsy.

Kind of like me.

"I love the collage background on this one," Felicia said. "It must have taken you a really long time."

I shrugged. "Not really," I lied. "No big deal."

"You are *so* talented, Amanda," Felicia said. "I bet you'll be a famous artist someday."

"Well, that's good," I tried to joke. "Because I guess my big career in politics is over."

Felicia frowned. "You should definitely think about this whole thing some more before you decide to quit," she said.

I hesitated. I could go over right now and toss my posters in the trash barrel at the end of the hall. So what if they were *artistic?*

Then I thought about the arts program I'd been planning to fight for. What would happen if Arielle won? All the money might end up going to the sports teams. And that wasn't fair.

It didn't matter how the posters looked, really. It was what they stood for. The ideas behind them. *My* ideas.

As I was standing there with Felicia, still holding

the posters, Dee Dee McKenzie came up to us. She didn't seem any more eager to go into homeroom than I was.

In fact, Dee Dee looked totally sad. Not her usual spunky self. Not the captain of the WLMS Spirit Squad. Usually she was in the middle of a whole group of kids. But not today.

"Dee Dee, what's wrong?" I asked, concerned. "Is everything okay?"

"Yes," she said. Then she looked down at the ground. "Well, actually . . . no."

"What happened?" Felicia asked her. "Is there anything we can do?"

Dee Dee shook her head. "No," she said. "It's no big deal, I guess. It's just that"—she took a deep breath— "Arielle Davis is running for class president now, too."

"Yeah, I heard that," I said. I almost made a smart crack about Arielle. But I thought maybe I should cheer up Dee Dee. "Hey, the more the merrier, right?" I added.

"Right," Felicia jumped in. "It'll be a really interesting election. Maybe having another candidate in the race will take some of the pressure off you and Amanda."

I nudged Felicia with my elbow. *I'm not running anymore, remember?* I wanted to say.

"No," Dee Dee said with a sigh. "It won't make any difference. I'm dropping out."

"What? That's crazy!" I cried. "You can't just quit!"

Felicia raised an eyebrow at me.

"Why not?" Dee Dee said. "Arielle Davis is, like, the most popular girl in sixth grade. Everybody knows her. Why should anyone else even bother running? She's practically won already. The whole school is talking about it."

Then Dee Dee stopped and clapped a hand over her mouth. "Oops," she said. "Sorry, Amanda. I didn't really mean that. I'm sure you have a great chance of winning, too."

Right, I thought. I knew Dee Dee was just trying to make me feel better.

But then I realized something. If I dropped out, Arielle would win. And not just the election. If I quit, I would be admitting to Arielle that she was right and I was wrong. Well, forget it.

I straightened my shoulders a little. I had to make this fast, because the late bell was going to ring in about one second.

"You're not dropping out, Dee Dee," I said firmly. "And neither am I. This election isn't over when Arielle Davis says it is. Or thinks it is. It's over when all the votes are counted and not a second earlier."

Felicia gave me a big smile and a thumbs-up.

Dee Dee hesitated. "Well . . ." she said slowly. "I don't know. . . ."

"You have to stand up for what you believe in," I

went on. "No matter what. Even if neither of us wins, our voices will have been heard."

Dee Dee didn't answer at first. Then she grinned. "Okay, Amanda," she said finally. "I hadn't really thought about it like that. But you're right. I'm staying in."

"Pretty impressive, Madam President," Felicia muttered under her breath.

Dee Dee and I shook hands just as Ms. McClintic came to the door. "Ladies," she said. "It's that time. Let's go."

Dee Dee threw me and Felicia a smile and hurried into her homeroom.

I turned to Felicia. "Yikes," I said. "You're going to be late. Sorry. But thanks."

"Sure," Felicia said. "That's what friends are for." She turned to go. "But Amanda, there is one thing."

"What?" I asked.

"Well," Felicia said, looking uncomfortable, "I'm afraid I'm not quite as brave as you are. And Arielle will be really mad at me if I support you in front of everybody."

"Oh," I said, shrugging. "That's okay. I understand." Actually, I couldn't help feeling a little disappointed that Felicia wasn't going to stand up for me. But at least she was still my friend.

"I mean, I didn't go to Quick-Os with her and Traci yesterday to have those posters made," Felicia added quickly. "And I didn't help them plan anything.

88

I just did . . . nothing." Felicia looked down at her yellow Skechers. "I'm such a wimp."

"No problem, Felicia," I told her. "And you're not a wimp. I'll deal with Arielle, okay? And you'd better get going or—"

I had barely started my last sentence when the bell interrupted me. Felicia gasped and took off down the hall.

"Bye!" I called after her. Then I lifted my chin and headed into homeroom.

It was time to face the music.

chapter
TEN

Sign posted inside WLMS Library

Students—SHHH!!! The library is not a social center. We expect your cooperation. NO talking, NO disruptive behavior, NO food, NO drinks, NO gum chewing, NO note passing, NO spitballs, NO writing in books.
Thank you, The Library Staff

(Scrawled note added by student)
NO BREATHING!!!!!

Arielle and Traci totally ignored me in homeroom.

But that was fine with me. I didn't want to talk to them, anyway. And I sure wasn't going to apologize again.

As soon as I sat down, I took out my purple notebook and began to draft my speech. It was a little hard to concentrate. But it helped that I'd already done some work on Friday night. And, of course, Asher had helped me on Saturday.

I made a note in the margin to tell him thank you

again. He probably thought I was pretty weird after I ran out of the pizza place like that.

I hardly listened as Ms. McClintic read the morning announcements. Then I heard her say, "And class officer candidates—Amanda, Dee Dee, Julie, Arielle—don't forget about your special meeting during sixth period."

Julie, I remembered, was running for class secretary. Dee Dee threw me a panicked "are-you-*sure*-you-want-to-go-through-with-this" look.

I smiled and gave her an encouraging thumbs-up.

Arielle was craning her head around the room, checking to make sure that everyone realized she was running now.

A few kids looked surprised. But most of them didn't. One boy called, "Way to go, Arielle!"

Ms. McClintic turned and frowned at him.

From across the room, Dee Dee frowned at me.

I frowned at the back of Arielle's head.

Bring it on, I told my ex–best friend silently. *Bring it on.*

At lunchtime I didn't bother going to the cafeteria. Maybe I should have gone around to all the tables, asking kids to vote for me. I'm sure that's what Arielle was doing. But I didn't feel like it right then.

Or maybe I just knew the truth. I couldn't beat Arielle by trying to be more popular than her. That was totally impossible.

My personality is fine, I think. I'm just . . . me. I get okay grades. People say I'm talented at art—and not just my friends. Penny calls me "naturally gifted." And

I always try to do what Adele refers to as "random acts of kindness." For people and animals.

Sure, I want kids to like me. But if they don't, I figure that's their problem.

Arielle is . . . well, Arielle. She's pretty and she's outgoing and she has supercool clothes. She's what my dad calls a "strong personality." She can twist her parents and teachers around her finger and make practically anyone laugh. Or cry.

She's also a really good friend. I mean, she *used* to be.

Like I said before, Arielle always gets what she wants. And if she doesn't, she always turns the situation around somehow. Crabby Aunt Delores, who's practically ancient, has this saying: "If life gives you lemons, make lemonade."

Well, Arielle is the Minute Maid queen.

But you know what? I could be, too. You can get whatever you want if you work hard enough. You just can't ever give up.

And right then I wanted to be class president. So I decided to skip lunch and use the extra hour to work on my debate notes.

Focus, focus, focus, I repeated to myself as I walked toward the library. That's what Traci always says.

I suddenly realized that in my mind I'd just quoted five different people in about five seconds. But maybe that's not so weird. It means I listen, I remember details, and I think about others' opinions.

Aha! More reasons to vote for me, Amanda Kepner. I stopped right there in the hallway and jotted them down quickly in my notebook.

That's when I heard Arielle's voice from across the hall. Loud and clear.

It seemed like she was everywhere today.

"So, anyway, we're definitely going to have a fall dance to raise money for our class," Arielle was telling a whole group of kids. "And after I win—I mean *if* I win, of course—I'm going to have a huge victory party. It's going to be at some really cool place. I haven't decided exactly where yet. But it'll be even bigger than that benefit party I had a month ago for the Wonder Lake Animal Shelter."

I flattened myself against a bank of lockers and gritted my teeth.

What did Arielle mean, the party *she* had for the shelter? She had a little help from her friends. Like me, Traci, and Felicia.

"The victory party will help raise money for a new program I started," Arielle went on. "It's called Healing Paws. Have you heard of it yet? We help sick kids in the hospital get well by bringing them cute animals to play with."

I was really steamed now. And I couldn't stand listening to Arielle for one more second. I pushed straight past the crowd of kids toward the double doors at the end of the hall. I didn't even care whether anyone saw me.

I guess no one did. I felt like the Invisible Candidate.

Then Arielle's voice carried down the hall. "That's because I care a lot about helping kids *and* animals. Unlike some *other* people."

I kept walking, focusing on the library doors.

How could Arielle be so incredibly mean to me? I'd made one tiny mistake. Told one little lie. I never meant to upset everyone like that. I'd even apologized to all my friends.

But Arielle didn't want to stop fighting. And this whole school election deal was making things even worse.

If I dropped out of the race, would Arielle forgive me? Would everything go back to normal with her and me and Traci and Felicia?

Somehow I had a feeling the answer was "no." To both questions. And right now, I didn't care whether all of us made up or not.

I wasn't quitting.

My stomach rumbled loudly as I pushed through the glass doors. I'd left my lunch back in my locker. There was no point in bringing it. Food wasn't allowed inside the library.

I walked over to one of the carrels just outside the reference area. No one would bother me there. That's where the geeks always sat.

Wasn't that what Arielle had called the kids who

got involved in student government? Except for Asher Bank. And now Arielle.

That thought made me mad all over again. I dropped my books a little too loudly on the desk.

The librarian at the reference desk cleared her throat. I sat down quickly.

The guy in the carrel next to me poked his head around the divider. Asher Bank. And I really didn't feel like seeing him right now. He reminded me of the whole mess I'd gotten into with my friends.

"Just wanted to see who was so ticked off," he whispered with a grin.

I sighed. "I guess you could say that," I told him.

"So how's it going?" Asher asked.

"Okay," I replied, shrugging. Then I remembered I was supposed to thank him again. "It was really nice of you to help me on Saturday. Sorry I had to leave like that."

"No problem," Asher said. Then he smiled. "Getting nervous, huh?"

"A little," I admitted. "I thought maybe I should make a few more notes for the debate. That's why I'm here right now."

"Nervous is good," Asher said. "That means you'll have extra adrenaline. Remember all those things we talked about, okay? You'll do great."

"Thanks," I said. Then I took a deep breath and got down to work.

I had just finished outlining the advantages of a student buddy system when Asher poked his head around again.

"Hey, Amanda," he said. "Does your friend Arielle have a boyfriend?"

I stiffened. *Arielle? Boyfriend?*

Why is he asking me that? I wondered. *He has a girlfriend!* Then I started thinking. . . . Was Asher planning on breaking up with his girlfriend to date Arielle? And was *that* why he was being so nice to me? Unbelievable!

"No," I told him shortly. "But I think maybe she's looking for one."

Like YOU, I added to myself.

The librarian cleared her throat again—loudly—so Asher didn't have a chance to answer.

For some reason, I thought of Dave. I hadn't seen him all day at school. Had Traci told him what really happened on Saturday?

I hoped not. I put my head in my hands and stared hard at my notebook. I couldn't think about Dave right now.

I needed to focus.

By the end of the period I managed to get a lot done. I hardly even noticed when Asher left. He just sort of tapped me on the shoulder on his way out.

As I was packing my stuff into my knapsack, Felicia came into the library.

"Hi," I said in surprise. I was really glad to see a friendly face. "What are you doing here? We're both supposed to go to earth science now."

"I know," Felicia said. "I thought I'd walk with you. I had a feeling you'd be hungry." She waved a bag of carrots. "I brought you a snack."

I grinned. "Felicia, you're a lifesaver."

Felicia frowned and dug around in her black bag. "Wait a sec. I might actually have some of those, too." With a triumphant look, she pulled out half a roll of hard candy. "Only ten calories apiece," she said.

I crunched on carrots and candy all the way to class. It wasn't my usual tomato and cheese with pickles, but they tasted pretty good. Besides, I could go to my locker and get my lunch after the candidates' meeting.

If I even feel like eating then, I thought. Listening to Arielle brag to everyone in the auditorium about her big campaign promises would probably make me sick. I mean, how many parties and dances could we have at WLMS? What about the really important stuff?

"I started to get a little worried when you didn't show up at lunch," Felicia said as we walked down the hall.

"I just thought it might be awkward," I told her. "You know, with Arielle and Traci and you in the middle of everything. And I didn't want to sit by myself."

"You wouldn't have to do that," Felicia said quickly. "I'm sure Arielle and Traci wouldn't mind."

I raised one eyebrow.

"Well, okay, maybe they're both still a little mad," Felicia said. "But they're all involved with Arielle's campaign stuff at the moment, so . . ." Her voice trailed off.

"Whatever," I said with a sigh. "I don't care that much, anyway. I'm totally busy with my campaign, too. That's the main reason I was in the library at lunch."

Felicia picked up the pace a little. Earth science was all the way at the end of the hall on the third floor, about as far from the library as you could get. Most of the kids had gone into their classrooms already. "Amanda, I'm telling you. There's no way you'd ever have to sit at a table by yourself," she said. "Even if Arielle and Traci were being mean. You have lots of other friends."

"Not good ones," I said with a bigger sigh.

Felicia stopped in her tracks. "Amanda, quit it!" she said. "Right now."

"Quit what?" I asked, puzzled. "The campaign?"

Felicia threw up her hands. "Here we go again," she said. "I give up. Where's the *real* Amanda Kepner? The one who refused to quit because of Arielle Davis? The one who told Dee Dee all that stuff about your voices being heard? The one who thinks ideas count? The one who has *guts?*"

Felicia did have a point. I was acting like a total wimp.

"What you need," Felicia went on, "is a little more confidence. You're never going to win if you keep acting like you lost your best friend."

I didn't answer. I just stared at the row of ugly

green lockers beyond Felicia's head. There was a serious dent in one of them.

"Oops," Felicia said. "Sorry, Amanda. I didn't mean that. I just meant—"

"That's okay," I broke in. "I know, I guess I've been feeling a little sorry for myself. I'll snap out of it. I promise."

"Well, you've got tons to offer," Felicia said. "But if you want to be class president, you're going to have to act like one. You can't let Arielle get to you. Politics is like chess or something. It's a game."

I grinned. "You know, Ms. Fiol, you may have a brilliant career in store at CNN."

Felicia grinned back. "Or maybe I could be some brilliant politician's campaign manager. But I'd need a little experience first."

My mouth dropped open. Was Felicia offering to help me?

"So how about it, Madam President-to-be? Do we have a deal?"

I hesitated. "What about Arielle?" I asked slowly. "She won't be happy about this at all."

"Well, for one thing, she might not even notice," Felicia said, shrugging. "She and Traci have been pretty absorbed the last couple of days. But the truth is, I can't tell you that you need to have more guts when I'm being a total wimp myself."

"Good point," I agreed. Then I stuck out my

hand. "All right, Madam Campaign Manager!"

The two of us giggled and headed into earth science together. And for the first time all day, I didn't feel like such a loser anymore.

I actually felt like a winner.

"Good luck with your campaign, Amanda," one girl said as I passed her desk. "My friend Lucy and I are going to vote for you."

I almost said, "You're kidding. Really?" But instead I just said, "Thanks, Gabby. That'd be great."

Thanks to Felicia, Gutsy Amanda was back!

After earth science, I had half an hour of Spanish to endure before the candidates' meeting.

Usually I love Spanish class. But it was hard to ignore Arielle and Traci. They kept passing notes to each other and whispering.

One of the notes fell right near my desk. I was tempted to pick it up and read it.

But I didn't. Gutsy Amanda didn't care what her ex-friends were saying about her.

At two twenty-five, Arielle and I were dismissed for the meeting.

Both of us were silent as we walked down the hall, side by side.

Arielle kept trying to get ahead of me. But I wouldn't let her. When she sped up, so did I.

The two of us were practically running by the time we reached the auditorium.

As soon as we got there, Arielle immediately began broadcasting her plans for a big fall dance again. Maybe she should have just grabbed the microphone to make her voice even louder.

I took a seat next to Dee Dee. She was biting her nails.

"I really have a bad feeling about this," she said. "Look at Arielle up there by the stage. She's the center of attention."

"Mmmm," I agreed. I wasn't going to let Dee Dee get me down. "Well, that's Arielle's style, I guess. So do you think you'll be ready for the debate?"

"I hope so," Dee Dee said. She brightened a little. "The Spirit Squad is going to help me. They're making up some really hard pretend questions for me to practice with. And we're all going to wear our uniforms in school that day."

"Sounds like a good plan," I said, nodding. I could tell that Dee Dee just wasn't into this whole election deal. But I wanted to be encouraging. I felt kind of responsible for talking her out of quitting. Maybe I shouldn't have done that. After all, it was Dee Dee's decision. Not mine.

Maybe I'd just wanted company up there on the stage when I went up against Arielle. And that wasn't right.

I was about to say something to Dee Dee when Asher stepped up to the podium.

"Let's call this meeting to order," he said. "Thank you for coming today. All of us in student government really appreciate your participation."

I could see why Asher got elected student council president. He was good. Really good. And he didn't seem nervous at all.

"The field of candidates is very impressive this year," Asher went on.

Arielle twisted around in her seat in the front row and gave everyone a gracious glance.

"But this year we're going to do things a little differently. Instead of the usual, and let's face it, *boring*, speeches"—everyone laughed—"a debate will be held on Friday for each group of class officer candidates."

Asher paused. "Three teachers will ask questions for the candidates to field," he continued. "There will be time for rebuttals and a short closing statement from each candidate at the end. The speeches on the day before the elections will be very brief. Five minutes max, just a final appeal for votes."

I made a few notes in my notebook. Was a debate better or worse than giving a whole speech? A debate was harder to prepare for, but if I was organized enough, I could work in some of the points I had planned to use in my speech. And it wasn't like the debate part was a surprise or anything.

I didn't know about Dee Dee, but this new format would probably work better for me than Arielle.

Long speeches had to be funny and entertaining. Debates were quick and to the point.

I glanced back at Arielle. She was whispering with a seventh-grade girl who was running for secretary.

The format doesn't matter, I told myself. *Remember the important thing: Issues, issues, issues.*

Like the arts program.

I might have to rethink my strategy a little. But with Felicia's help, I could do it.

Gutsy Amanda was determined to win, no matter what.

And maybe, just maybe, she would.

chapter
ELEVEN

Notes for D(ebate) DAY

ARTS FUNDING—SUPER IMPT.!!
6TH/8TH GRADE BUDDY PROGRAM
FUND-RAISER IDEAS (PANCAKE BREAKFAST?
STUDENT/TEACHER BASKETBALL GAME?)
ADD ARTS SECTION TO SCHOOL PAPER
SUGGESTION BOX OUTSIDE STUDENT
GOVERNMENT OFFICE

Fall Dance!!!!
Raise more $$$$ for sports teams (esp. soccer!)—
new uniforms a MUST!
Pump up school spirit with more parties!
Stereo system for cafeteria? Student DJs?
Convince Mom I need highlights before Friday!

I didn't see much of Arielle and Traci for the next few
days. In homeroom and our classes the two of them
just kept ignoring me.

Hey, I didn't care. *Really.*

Felicia and I spent a lot of time together planning our campaign strategy. I wanted to keep everything really low-key. But Felicia convinced me that I had to make myself more visible.

"You have to make a statement," she insisted. "A strong one."

On Thursday morning Felicia was waiting for me when I got off the bus. She was holding a plastic bag from a funky store at the mall, Button Up.

"Have a button," she told the girl in front of me.

The girl took the button and fastened it to her denim jacket. "Hey, cool," the girl said. "Thanks."

The button was purple with neon green letters. It said: VOTE SMART. VOTE KEPNER. That was the campaign slogan Felicia and I had come up with on Tuesday night. I actually liked it a lot. Short and to the point.

"Wow," I said to Felicia. "Those look great. But—"

Felicia kept handing out buttons to every kid who came off the bus. "Shhh," she told me. "Don't talk to me. Talk to them!"

I wasn't sure I wanted everyone wearing Kepner buttons. It seemed a little . . . tacky. But no one seemed to mind.

"Hi, I'm Amanda," I said with a smile as I handed a button to a boy from my earth science class. "I hope you'll vote for me on election day!"

He smiled back. "Hey, I'm Jack. Did you make all of your posters yourself?"

I blushed. "Yeah, most of them."

"You're really talented! No wonder you're so into the arts program. Anyway, good luck." He waved and headed off.

I looked at Felicia in wonder.

"See?" she said excitedly. "Handing out the buttons gives you a chance to talk to people. And when you talk to people, you get votes."

I nodded. "I guess so."

Even the two girls who had told me they were voting for Dee Dee took buttons. "Good luck," Sandy told me over her shoulder.

I shrugged. "I don't believe it," I said to Felicia.

"Everyone likes to get free stuff," Felicia pointed out. "Hey, wait a minute. You need a button, too." She reached out and pinned one to my tie-dyed T-shirt.

I felt like I had a huge sign blinking on my chest. Sort of like Arielle's pink banner, which was still hanging in the lobby. "What's next?" I joked to Felicia. "Sandwich boards?"

Felicia thought for a minute. "Mmmm. No. Not your style."

"I wasn't being serious," I said. I smiled and nodded to a boy from my Spanish class. "*Hola*," I greeted him.

Soon the whole bag of buttons was gone.

"I brought something else, too," Felicia said. "You'll see it on the way into school."

It was a huge VOTE KEPNER banner—tied in the branches of the big maple tree. *Our* maple tree.

I stared at the sign in horror. Felicia had made it out of a big white sheet. The letters were spray-painted in purple. I didn't want to hurt her feelings, but . . .

"Um, don't you think maybe it's a little big?" I asked doubtfully.

"No," Felicia said. "It's part of your statement. You know: big, bold, confident."

"Right," I said. Then I squinted up into the tree more closely. "You didn't use tacks to fasten that sheet, did you?"

Felicia laughed. "No, Amanda," she said again. "I knew you were going to ask me that. No trees were harmed in the making of this banner. It's tied. See the rope? Dave helped me put it up really early this morning."

"Dave McClintic?" I asked in surprise.

"Of course," Felicia said. "How many other Daves do we know? Traci's brother. Your future husband."

I could feel myself blushing. "Oh," I said. Then I frowned. "Wait a second. He's *not* my future husband."

Felicia just smiled knowingly. "If you say so," she answered.

I had only seen Dave a few times in the hall this week. And once coming out of the cafeteria. He'd

107

smiled and said hi to me, just like he always did. But I still didn't know. . . .

"Felicia, did Traci ever tell Dave about . . . last weekend?" I asked. "Because I wouldn't want him to think that Asher and I were on a date or anything."

"So you *do* care about Dave," Felicia teased.

I looked down at the ground. "Well, yeah. I mean, it's not like we're going to go out—he's two years older than me. And Traci would have a fit, anyway."

Felicia shrugged. "Well, you never know. She might be okay with it. But to answer your question, no. The last I knew, Traci hadn't told Dave anything about what really happened on Saturday."

I breathed a sigh of relief. "Good," I said. "I was kind of worried that he'd hate me."

"Are you kidding?" Felicia cried. "Haven't you noticed the way the poor guy looks at you? He's so obviously in love."

"I think that's pushing it a little, Felicia," I said. "Maybe he *likes* me. Kind of."

Felicia threw up her hands. "You're impossible, Amanda," she said.

"No," I said. "I'm just . . . low-key."

"Whatever," Felicia said with a sigh.

"By the way, Asher has a girlfriend," I told her. "Did you know that? He mentioned her when we were talking on the phone Friday night."

"I had no idea," Felicia replied. Then she looked

worried. "And I don't think Arielle knows it, either. I've seen her talking to him a few times. She has a major crush on him."

"Yeah, so I figured," I said. "But the weird thing is, he was asking me whether she had a boyfriend. So I don't know *what's* going on."

Felicia frowned. "You think he's going to break up with his girlfriend? Are you going to tell Arielle?"

I shrugged. "I'm not really in a position to tell her."

"Me neither," Felicia answered in a small voice. "Arielle and I aren't exactly on speaking terms right now."

"You're not?" I asked. "What happened?" But I had a feeling I knew the answer to that one. It was all my fault.

Felicia shrugged. "Well, I told her I was helping you with your campaign. You know, like Traci was helping her. And just like you thought, she wasn't very happy about it at all."

"Oh no," I said. "I'm so sorry, Felicia. I should never have let you be my campaign manager. Even though you're doing such a great job," I added quickly.

"Don't be sorry," Felicia told me. "I really like Arielle. But I won't let her bully me. I have the right to make up my own mind about who to vote for. I happen to agree with you about the arts program funding. And like I said before, I think all your ideas are great. I know this election is really important to you, Amanda. And so is Healing Paws, no matter what Arielle says. I don't care if she's mad at me. I'm still going to help you."

"Thanks," I said. "You're a true friend." Then I grinned. "Hey, that was a pretty long speech. Are you sure *you* don't want to run for president?"

Felicia grinned back. "No way," she said. "I'm a total wimp, remember?"

"No," I told her seriously. "You're not a wimp. In fact, I think Wimpy Felicia could beat Gutsy Amanda any day."

Just then Arielle swept up beside us. For once she was alone. She was wearing her soccer jersey over designer jeans. Today was a game day for her and Traci.

"Well, well," she said. "If it isn't the Traitor and the Sneak."

That was the most Arielle had said to me in three days.

Felicia opened her mouth, then closed it again. She looked hurt.

I didn't reply, either. There was no point in stooping to Arielle's level. Which was pretty low, if you ask me.

Arielle looked up at the Vote Kepner banner. "Not bad," she said. "Gee, I hope it doesn't rain today. It would be terrible if all the letters ran." She looked up pointedly at the sky.

Felicia and I followed her gaze. Sure enough, the sky looked really cloudy. It was probably going to start pouring any second now.

"That's okay," Felicia said evenly. "Everyone's already seen it."

Arielle gave her a steely look. "Whatever," she said. Then she turned and stomped off toward the school building.

"She sure is mad." Felicia shook her head. "I've never seen her like this."

"Well, I have," I told her. "Plenty of times, starting from first grade. Don't worry, she'll get over it. Eventually."

"Even if she loses the election?" Felicia asked.

I frowned. Actually, I wasn't so sure about that. As far as I knew, Arielle had never lost anything. Ever.

"Sure," I said with a casual wave. I tried to sound extra-confident for Felicia's sake. "Arielle will bounce back like a rubber ball."

But I had a feeling that wasn't exactly true. A cannonball was more like it.

After gym class that afternoon, I went to my locker to get the new posters I'd made the night before. They weren't quite as nice as the ones I'd worked on over the weekend. That's because I didn't have as much time. But they looked okay.

Felicia had made more posters for me, too, besides the banner. I felt like my name was plastered all over the school now.

I needed all the PR I could get. Every vote was going to count.

Arielle hadn't bothered to put up any more posters. She was talking to kids instead. In the halls, in the cafeteria, on the front lawn, on the soccer field, in the band room, even in the library. Arielle seemed to be in a zillion places at once. By now she'd probably reached every sixth grader at WLMS. Everyone was talking about the fall dance she was promising.

Big deal.

Just as I got to my locker, I saw Traci. She was at her own locker, a few down from mine. And she was having trouble pulling something out from the top. It was crammed with junk. Books, notebooks, papers, soccer cleats, a water bottle, a bike helmet . . .

"Yikes!" Traci cried suddenly.

She put her arms over her head to shield herself as all of the stuff came tumbling down.

I ran over to help. "Hold still," I told her.

I caught an extra-heavy textbook just as it was about to hit Traci on the head.

"*Principles of Science*," I said, reading the cover. "Ouch."

"Thanks," Traci told me, wiping her brow. "Phew! That was close."

"Principle of science number one," I said. "No object can resist the pull of gravity."

Traci grinned. Then she seemed to catch herself. "Funny," she muttered. Then she stooped to gather up all the junk on the floor.

I knelt beside her. "I'll help you put this stuff back in your locker if you want," I offered.

Traci hesitated. "That'd be great," she said finally. "I'm going to be late for soccer practice. Coach will have a fit. I'm starting in the game today for Arielle."

Together we put each item carefully back in Traci's locker.

"Maybe the bike helmet should go in the bottom part," I suggested.

"Good idea," Traci said, wedging it in behind her Muskrats jacket.

Now it was my turn to hesitate. "Um, Traci, I know you're in a hurry," I said. "Can I walk to the gym with you?"

Traci shut her locker and gave the lock a twist. She didn't look at me. "I guess," she said.

"Listen, Traci," I began as we headed down the hall. *What was I going to say?* "I'm really, really sorry about what happened last weekend. And I want us to be friends again."

There, I thought. Short and to the point.

But Traci didn't answer. She just kept walking.

"Hey, guys." It was Dave, straightening up from the drinking fountain.

"Hi," Traci said shortly.

"Hi," I said. "How's it going?"

"Not too bad," Dave answered. He quickly wiped

the water that was dripping off his chin. "How's the big campaign?"

"Okay, I guess," I said. "Thanks for—" I hesitated. Should I mention his helping Felicia hang the VOTE KEPNER banner in the tree? Did Traci know about that? I didn't want her mad at Dave, too.

"Everything," I finished lamely. Traci looked confused.

"Sure," Dave said. "Well, I'd better go," he said. "I've got an algebra quiz next period." He waved and loped off down the hall.

Traci turned to me. "Okay, Amanda," she said. "I've got to know. Do you like my brother or not? Spill it."

I drew back. "Wh-what are you talking about?" I asked, trying to stall for time. How should I answer? Either way, I was cooked.

"My brother *really* likes you, Amanda," Traci said. "And it's not fair for you to act like you have a crush on him if you really don't."

I gazed up at the VOTE SMART. VOTE KEPNER. poster on the wall behind Traci's head. What was the smart answer here?

I remembered what Penny had said about lying: It always comes back to you.

I had no choice. I'd have to tell Traci the truth.

"I—I do like Dave," I said finally. "A lot. He's cute. And nice. And funny. And, um, sweet."

Traci snorted. "Ha," she muttered.

I braced myself. But Traci didn't seem mad. In fact, she was actually smiling now.

"No need to go overboard," she said. "He's my *brother*, remember?"

I smiled back. "Sorry," I told her.

The two of us started walking again. "I should get to practice now," Traci said, frowning. "I've been late the last couple of times."

I nodded. "We can talk later, I guess."

"Sure," Traci said. "But I'm still backing Arielle." She gave me a meaningful look. "I have to support the sports program. And, um . . ." Traci looked around and leaned in close to me, then whispered, "If the arts program loses funding . . . maybe it'll get me out of orchestra."

I looked at Traci to see if she was kidding, but she looked serious. "You really hate it, huh?"

Traci sighed. "I hate messing up. It's hard enough to mess up in front of the kids, but to disappoint my own mother . . ." She shook her head. Ms. McClintic was the orchestra leader, in addition to being our homeroom teacher.

"Don't you guys have a competition coming up?" I asked.

Traci nodded. "Regional finals," she said. "If we win, we get to go to the state semifinals in Chicago."

"Wow," I said. "That would be great for you."

"Yeah," said Traci, looking depressed. "And if I make us lose, it could be pretty miserable."

115

I looked at Traci. She looked so sad, I could actually understand why she was voting for Arielle.

"Okay," I said. "No hard feelings."

And that was the truth. Just like Felicia, Traci had a right to vote for anyone she wanted.

I was just happy to have my friend back again.

Two down.

One more to go.

chapter
TWELVE

Note passed to Amanda on the bus

Amanda,
**   I asked Lucy to give this to you for me. I told Asher today I had to quit. EVERYONE'S voting for Arielle! Even some of the kids from Spirit Squad. So I just can't go through with it. I'm really sorry. I might go for VP instead.**

**   Luv, DDMcK**
P.S. I promise I'll vote for you!

I set my alarm for six A.M. on the morning of D day.

Debate day.

Doomsday.

No, I thought. *Believe in yourself. Confidence breeds more confidence.*

Who was I quoting now? I had no idea.

Probably Felicia. She'd been surfing the Net for me last night, looking for articles on conquering nervousness.

I picked out my clothes carefully: my favorite purple

suede skirt and a purple blouse with funky little shapes all over it. It was the sort of outfit I usually wore to church or to visit Aunt Delores. But it was pretty much all I had besides jeans and what Arielle always calls my "hippie clothes."

Besides, purple was my lucky color.

I hoped.

I spotted Arielle as soon as I got off the bus. She was dressed in a navy blazer and a short plaid skirt. She looked almost like a miniversion of her lawyer mom, but a lot cooler. Her newly highlighted auburn hair was shining in the early autumn sun.

I had to hand it to Arielle. She looked so . . . professional. Like Reese Witherspoon in that movie *Election.* I expected her to start giving her acceptance speech right there on the front lawn.

"Hi," I heard Arielle greeting a group of kids as I got closer. "How's it going? You're voting for me next week, right?"

I don't think she saw me. She was too busy handing out red-white-and-blue GET IN THE SPIRIT WITH ARIELLE! buttons to half the world.

What a copycat. I gave out buttons, so she had to do the same thing. Except Arielle's buttons were a lot bigger than mine. Probably more expensive, too. I'd paid Felicia back twenty-five dollars from my hard-earned allowance.

But that was money down the drain now.

Practically all the kids from our class were gathered around Arielle.

Okay, maybe I was exaggerating a bit.

I couldn't ignore the truth, though. Arielle's strategy was working. Everyone was trying to get her attention and fastening on their buttons.

"Vote Davis if you want a sixth-grade dance!" she called after some other kids passing by.

I sighed and hurried quickly past the Arielle fan club. I wanted to get inside the building and start going over my notes for the debate as soon as I could.

Luckily the debates were being held first thing in the morning. That way, at least they'd be over with fast. I wouldn't have as much time to get nervous.

I already *was* nervous, actually. I'd gone over every possible question I might be asked about five thousand times in my head. Felicia had drilled me again and again with the flash cards I'd made.

I couldn't help wondering whether Arielle was nervous, too. It sure hadn't looked like it back there on the lawn.

I went straight to the auditorium and sat down in the front row to go over my notes. The kids wouldn't be coming in for the assembly for at least twenty minutes.

Asher was up on the stage, adjusting the microphones. I watched him for a while, glad for the distraction. I couldn't decide whether I was angry with him or not. On the one hand, he'd lied to me, saying he had a girlfriend. Or maybe he really did have a girlfriend. And he was planning to dump his girlfriend for Arielle.

Fine, I thought. *The two of them will make a great couple.*

On the other hand, Asher had been really nice to me. He'd helped me a lot. He'd even given up part of his weekend to meet with me.

It didn't make sense.

Maybe I was wrong somehow about Asher having a girlfriend. Maybe I hadn't heard him right over the phone.

I decided to give the guy the benefit of the doubt.

"Careful of those wires!" I called.

Asher saw me and waved. "Hey, don't worry. I learned my lesson, believe me." He jumped down from the stage and came to sit beside me. "So, are you ready?" he asked.

"I guess," I told him. "I'm still a little nervous."

"Just remember all the stuff we talked about on Saturday," Asher told me. "And you'll be fine."

"I sure hope so," I said.

"Piece of cake," Asher said with a grin. "And don't forget that very important warning I gave you. Whatever you do, *don't* imagine the audience sitting out here in their underwear."

Just the thought of that crazy idea made me smile in spite of myself. I didn't care anymore whether Asher was interested in Arielle or not. It wasn't any of my business, really. He was just a nice guy.

But I still liked Dave better.

Luckily Dave wouldn't be out in the audience this morning. The eighth graders had voted for their class officers last spring. So even if I made a total fool of myself, Dave wouldn't find out about it. Unless Traci told him. But somehow I had a feeling she wouldn't. We hadn't finished our talk from yesterday yet, but things seemed to be okay between us now. Maybe she wasn't thrilled that Dave and I liked each other. But I guess she wanted us both to be happy.

A bunch of other kids from student government walked into the auditorium. Asher quickly got up from his seat. "Gotta go, Amanda," he said. "Good luck, okay?"

"Thanks," I told him. For a second I wondered whether he was going to tell Arielle the same thing. Was he hoping she'd win the debate?

But I quickly realized how stupid that was. Of course Asher should wish Arielle luck, too. All the candidates should do a good job.

Speaking of other candidates, I suddenly realized that they had already arrived in the auditorium. We were supposed to be there ahead of everyone else. The homerooms were coming at nine-thirty.

It was nine-twenty now. And I hadn't gone over my notes at all.

"Okay, guys," Cassandra Jackson called. "Everybody take your places up here onstage. Each chair has a name on a piece of masking tape. Let's roll."

My heart started to race so fast, I thought I was going to faint.

I stood up to walk to the stage, but my heart was pounding so much, I had to sit back down. Nobody saw me. Except Arielle. Now she knew I was really nervous.

She gave me a funny look and turned away. But it wasn't a mean look. It was more of a *worried* look.

I suddenly felt a little better. My heart had slowed from its Indy 500 pace. I stood up again and gathered my index cards. I wanted to keep them out in case I needed to look at them while I was speaking.

I also located a pen and tested it out on my arm to make sure it still worked. I might want to take notes. That's what the presidential candidates always did on TV.

I hurried up on the stage just as the auditorium doors opened. All of the homerooms started noisily filing in.

"Quiet, please, people," I heard my math teacher say. "This is a serious assembly."

I gulped. *That's for sure*, I thought.

It wasn't too hard to find my seat. It was the only empty one left. Right next to Arielle.

Of course.

Arielle gave me a sideways glance as I sat down and smoothed my skirt.

"Are you okay?" she asked.

"Yes," I answered. "Fine."

Arielle nodded slightly. She didn't say anything else.

At least she asked, I told myself. Arielle knew that heart-racing thing always scared me.

Is Arielle nervous, too? I wondered.

She didn't look it. In fact, she seemed cool as a cucumber, as Aunt Delores would say.

The three teachers who would give us the debate questions were taking their seats at a long table set up in front of the stage. The table held three microphones. Mr. Ellis, whom I had for earth science, was one of the teachers. And Ms. Petrocelli from English. And—Mrs. Papaleo, who gave drawing and ceramics classes.

Mrs. Papaleo smiled at me. I was one of her best students.

There were two podiums for the candidates, each with its own microphone. I was glad Arielle and I wouldn't have to share. There were only two of us running for sixth-grade class president.

That's when I noticed that there was only one candidate running for vice president of our class.

It was Dee Dee!

She leaned over and whispered, "Good luck."

"You too," I said.

"I'm a write-in," she told me. "It was Asher's suggestion. No one else wanted to run for VP."

Well, that was one way to win. "Congratulations," I whispered back.

"I just have to give my closing statement," Dee Dee said. "And the short speech next week. Not bad, huh?" She waved at a group of girls in the front row. They waved back. They were all dressed in blue-and-white WLMS Spirit Squad uniforms.

Kids were waving to Arielle, too. And shouting. "Whoo-hoo, Davis!" someone called. "Way to go!"

"Good luck, Arielle!" a girl from her soccer team called. "Go, Muskrats!"

Somewhere a kid whistled. One of the teachers immediately shushed him.

My heart was starting to race again.

Then I saw Felicia out in the audience.

She was wearing all purple, just like me.

And she was totally covered in VOTE KEPNER buttons.

That was so sweet. And funny. I started laughing.

Felicia gave me a little wave and a thumbs-up. Beside her, Dave held up a VOTE KEPNER sign.

Dave? What was he doing here? He was supposed to be back in his eighth-grade homeroom. What if he saw me totally screw up?

I smiled back at my friends. I had to admit seeing them there made me feel a whole lot better.

Then Asher Bank stepped to the podium and tapped on the microphone. "May I have your attention, please?" he said. "We're about to start the Wonder Lake Middle School election debates."

The auditorium grew quiet. I searched the sea of

faces and found Felicia again. She looked totally calm. She wasn't even biting her pinky fingernail.

What was it she had said about politics being a chess game?

Well, I was as ready as I'd ever be.

Let the game begin.

chapter
THIRTEEN

Scrawled on girls' room stall

IF YOU'RE READING THIS, U R A LOSER!!!!!!!

"Dee Dee McKenzie," Asher announced.

Asher had already introduced the three teachers who would be giving us the debate questions. Now he was presenting the sixth-grade candidates.

He had started with secretary. Then treasurer. Then vice president.

There was a burst of applause as Dee Dee stood up. The Spirit Squaders in the front row went wild.

Dee Dee smiled and waved. She was dressed all in blue and white. There was even a tiny blue-and-white shamrock in greasepaint on her cheek.

Dee Dee looked like her old self again. I was really happy for her.

"Puh-leez," I heard Arielle mutter under her breath. "Sit down already."

"And now for the two candidates for sixth-grade class president," Asher said. "First, Amanda Kepner."

I stood up, sending the index cards on my lap fluttering to the floor.

I heard some boy say, "Hey, look! It's snowing—note cards!"

My face flamed. But suddenly everyone was clapping for me. "Knock 'em dead, Amanda!" another guy called.

Was it Dave? I couldn't be sure.

From somewhere in the auditorium, I definitely heard Traci give her trademark earsplitting whistle. Usually I hate it when she does that.

But not today. It was nice to know she was supporting me. Even if she was going to vote for Arielle.

I sat down quickly and the auditorium grew silent. I tried to gather my note cards together as best I could using my feet.

"And Arielle Davis," Asher announced.

This time the applause was thunderous. I could feel the stage shaking under my chair.

All the kids were clapping and cheering and calling Arielle's name. Then they started stamping their feet on the floor in unison. "FALL DANCE, FALL DANCE, FALL DANCE!!!" they shouted.

I froze in my chair. This was even worse than I expected.

They loved Arielle.

They must hate me.

Arielle rose to her feet, beaming, and gave a little curtsy as a joke. People cheered even louder.

"Okay," Asher said into the microphone. "Thanks, everybody. It's time to get started."

The audience kept on clapping. Arielle kept on waving, egging them on.

Asher leaned into the microphone again. "If this assembly goes long, it will cut into our lunch period," he said.

That did it.

Everyone shut up, and Arielle sat down.

The other candidates, for secretary and treasurer, went first. I hardly listened to the debates. I tried to, I really did. I wanted to get a feel for the whole thing so it would be easier when it was my turn. But I was *way* too nervous to concentrate.

In the chair beside me, I could feel Arielle beginning to fidget. Was she actually getting nervous now, too?

Or was she just impatient for her turn in the spotlight?

Quit it, I scolded myself. That was mean. Even if no one else could hear what I was thinking, Arielle was my best friend. Or she used to be, anyway. How could our friendship have ended like this? We were still the same people, right?

Why were we running against each other?

That's Arielle's fault, Gutsy Amanda reminded me. *Forget about her. Get yourself together.*

I was so busy thinking about Arielle and me that I was totally startled when Asher called our names.

Oh no! I told myself. This was it. The big moment

I'd been waiting for—and preparing for—all week.

Everyone clapped, politely this time, as Arielle and I took our places at the podium.

Mr. Ellis didn't waste any time. "We'll start with you, Ms. Kepner," he said. "Why do you think you'd be a good class president?"

That was an easy one. The practice question I'd put down first on flash card number one.

But for the life of me, I couldn't think of the answer I'd prepared.

I glanced down at my note cards, but they were all mixed up now. I was going to have to wing it. And now I couldn't seem to find my voice, either. My heart started that crazy racing again.

"I—"

Then I saw Felicia. She was smiling at me encouragingly. Beside her, Dave held up his sign again. He must have flipped it over, because this time it said GO FOR IT, AMANDA!!!

I took a deep breath. "I'm a creative thinker," I said. "I really care about our school and I believe that no matter how differently we may think sometimes, there is always a way to compromise."

I paused. *Slow down*, I told myself. Asher had warned me about talking too fast.

"We have a great sixth-grade class this year, and I promise you that I will really work hard to make us even better," I went on. "Even though students don't make the final decisions on things, what we think is still important. The teachers and parents and administration listen to the opinions of our student government. And I would like to be one of your representatives."

"Your minute is up, Ms. Kepner," Mr. Ellis said. "Ms. Davis, same question. Why do you feel that you would be a good president?"

Arielle tapped on the microphone a few times to test it. Then she smiled at the crowd.

"I'm Arielle Davis," she said. "I'll be a fantastic class president because I know exactly what the students want. Yeah, schoolwork and grades are important. But what we need at WLMS is more school spirit. More *fun*, so that we can take a break from all the hard work we do."

Kids started cheering again, even though they weren't supposed to.

"Please hold your applause until the end," Asher told them.

"And we especially need an even stronger sports program," Arielle went on. "All of our teams are great—especially the soccer team—"

All the WLMS Muskrats cheered.

"—but we could be even better, with more money and new uniforms."

More applause. I felt my heart sinking.

"And most important," Arielle continued, "we need to have a lot more parties and dances. We can raise lots of money for our class and—"

"Thank you, Ms. Davis," Ms. Petrocelli broke in. "But your time is up."

Everyone booed. "Davis, Davis!" they chanted.

The rest of the debate was a blur.

Just as Asher had advised me, I answered each question in a way in which I could get my major ideas across. I remember talking about the importance of having a strong arts program at WLMS. And my idea for a monthly assembly so we could get to know our teachers better. And the new student buddy system. And everything else I'd thought of over the last week or so.

On the other hand, Arielle talked about the fall dance. A lot. And the sports program. Pretty much all the things she said when she answered the first question.

I wasn't sure, but I thought I saw Mrs. Papaleo smile at me as I sat back down. At least someone else thought the arts program was important. Even if it was just a teacher.

"We're going to give the candidates a quick break," Asher said. "We'll have the closing statements in about five minutes."

"What about lunch?" someone called. "I'm starving!"

Asher laughed. "Keep your pants on! It won't be long now. See you in five minutes."

The stage curtain closed in front of us. "Davis, Davis, Davis!!!" we heard kids chanting.

Arielle jumped up and went outside the curtain to greet her public.

I stared down at the note cards in my lap. I felt so totally stupid. No one cared about ideas. Why had I ever thought they would?

Arielle had already won.

Suddenly I felt a huge lump welling up in my throat. My eyes filled with tears.

This time it was me who jumped up from my chair. I ran straight for the girls' room backstage and locked myself into one of the stalls.

Everyone loved Arielle. They hated me. They hadn't even listened to my ideas.

I'm a total loser, I told myself.

Then the tears came. And they wouldn't stop.

chapter FOURTEEN

Sign Posted in the WLMS Cafeteria

Don't "Leave" Today Without
Buying Your Ticket for the
SIXTH-GRADE FALL DANCE!!!
Support the WLMS Arts Program
Cold Drinks, Hot Tunes, and Good Friends
You'll Be Blown Away!

"Amanda?"

Someone was knocking on the bathroom stall door. But I was crying so hard, I didn't realize it at first.

Then I saw a flash of blue-and-white shamrock underneath the stall door.

It was Dee Dee, trying to get my attention.

"Amanda, are you okay?" she asked, sounding concerned.

I leaned back against the stall and hugged myself closer. "I'm f-fine," I told her, sniffling. "Just a little . . . upset."

"You did really great out there," Dee Dee said. "Why are you crying?"

"Because Arielle won," I said in a small voice.

"No, she didn't," Dee Dee told me. "Not yet, anyway."

"Unless you quit," another voice added.

Felicia's face was next to Dee Dee's now. The two of them were upside down and frowning.

"How did you know I was here?" I asked Felicia, wiping my nose.

"I went back to see you after they closed the curtain," Felicia answered. "Arielle told me you'd disappeared. And as your campaign manager, I have to tell you that crying is not good for your presidential image."

"You were fantastic, I swear," Dee Dee said. "Everyone is talking about you and all your great ideas."

"No, they're not," I said. "They're talking about the fall dance. And how great Arielle Davis is."

"Okay, that's it," Felicia said. She crawled underneath the stall door and squeezed in beside me. Then she stood up and unlocked the door. "The pity party is over. Outside, Madam President. Now."

"But I don't want to," I whined.

Felicia reached down and helped me up. "Amanda, please. You have two minutes left before closing statements. Move."

"But—"

"No buts," Felicia said firmly. She practically pushed me out the door. "Where is your self-esteem? You have more confidence than anyone I've ever known. Even Arielle. She's not as tough as she looks. It's all an act."

"It's true," Dee Dee said, nodding.

"Wait a minute," I protested. "I've known Arielle forever. She has tons of confidence."

Felicia put her hands on her hips. "And why do you think that is?"

I hesitated. "Well . . . I guess . . . I have no idea."

"Because of *you*," Felicia said. "Think about it. Aren't you always there, supporting her? Telling her when she's wrong? Helping her out when she's in a jam?"

"Yeeees," I said slowly. "Sometimes."

"No, all the time," Felicia said. "The two of you are a team."

"Not anymore," I said sadly.

"All candidates back onstage!" someone called from the hallway. "They're about to raise the curtain!"

"We've got to go, Amanda," Dee Dee said. "Come on."

"I've got to go, too," Felicia said. "My homeroom teacher will be looking for me. But I'll see you afterward, okay?"

I nodded. Felicia and Dee Dee were really good friends. I wasn't sure I deserved them at the moment.

It ain't over till the fat lady sings, I told myself. That's one of my dad's favorite expressions. I was going to have to finish the race.

At least Felicia would vote for me. And Dee Dee.

"You go on ahead," I told them. "I'm just going to throw some water on my face. The treasurer and secretary candidates are giving their closing statements first. I'll have time."

"Well, okay," Felicia said reluctantly. "Good luck, Amanda."

"See you up onstage," Dee Dee called over her shoulder.

After they left, I walked over to one of the sinks and turned on the cold water faucet. Then I looked in the mirror.

I was a wreck. My eyes were swollen and my whole face was puffy.

Then, all of a sudden, I saw Arielle standing behind me.

"I figured you were in here," she said. "Listen, it'll be okay. But they need us out there. Come on, I'll walk back with you."

I looked at her suspiciously. Was Arielle being *nice* all of a sudden?

Arielle sighed. "Amanda, we're going to miss the whole thing." She reached over and pushed back my hair, hooking it behind my ears. "Everyone's waiting for us."

I held on to the sink with both hands. "I'm coming," I said. "Soon."

Arielle sighed and turned back to the door. "Well, good luck, Amanda Panda," she said. "You did a great job out there earlier."

Then she was gone.

I stared into the mirror again. Where was Gutsy Amanda when I needed her?

That's when I realized she was exactly where she belonged.

With me.

I ran out of the bathroom and made it onto the stage just as the curtain was rising. Arielle and I didn't say a word as we sat waiting for our turns. We didn't look at each other, either. But Arielle reached over and squeezed my hand. After a minute, I squeezed back.

For some reason, I felt a lot less nervous now.

We both gave our closing statements. They were pretty much the same as the answers we'd given to the "Why do you think you'd make a good president?" question. Asher had told me to make the same points in my closing as I had in my opening. Something about repetition being a good campaign tool.

Well, one thing was for sure. I'd given this whole election thing my best shot.

Asher walked to the podium. "We have one more closing statement," he told the audience.

I frowned and looked around. There weren't any more candidates left. We'd already done secretary, treasurer, and president.

"She doesn't have an opponent in her race, but she'd like to say a few words, anyway," Asher went on. "So please give a big hand for your new sixth-grade vice president, Dee Dee McKenzie."

Dee Dee! Of course. I'd forgotten she was supposed to give a closing statement, too.

Everyone clapped as Dee Dee walked to the podium. The Spirit Squaders jumped up and did a little dance behind the judges' table. One of them even did a cartwheel.

"Hi," Dee Dee said. "Well, I guess you all know who I am now. And you're not getting much choice about your vice president. It looks like you're stuck with me."

A few kids laughed good-naturedly.

"Anyway, I wanted to tell you that I'm really looking forward to representing all of you and working with everyone on the student council."

Dee Dee paused and looked around the auditorium. "But there's something else I'd like to say. Because you *do* have a choice for your president."

I almost fell off my chair. What was Dee Dee doing?

"As a lot of you know, I'm captain of the sixth-grade Spirit Squad."

The Squaders stood up and cheered again until Mrs. Papaleo shushed them.

"What you may not know is that I was planning to run for sixth-grade president." She took a deep breath. "But I didn't have the guts to go up against two great candidates. Arielle Davis and Amanda Kepner."

Arielle and I exchanged glances. "I don't believe this," Arielle whispered.

"Me neither," I whispered back.

The auditorium was totally silent now. Everyone seemed to be in shock.

"Both Arielle and Amanda would be great choices," Dee Dee said. "Don't get me wrong. But I'd like to tell you something about one of them."

This time Dee Dee paused for what seemed like a very long time. "Amanda Kepner has more school spirit than anyone else at WLMS," she said. "Maybe she doesn't show it the way some people do. She's not out there jumping up and cheering. But she really cares. About our school. And about her friends."

Mr. Ellis called Asher over and whispered something to him.

Asher just shook his head and shrugged.

"Please finish up, Ms. McKenzie," Mrs. Papaleo called. "We're almost out of time."

Dee Dee nodded. "Well, anyway," she rushed on, "I don't think I'd even be up here right now if it weren't for Amanda Kepner. And I'd like to ask anyone who would have voted for me to vote for her."

For a long second it seemed like no one was even breathing. Especially me. Then suddenly everyone started to clap and shout louder than they had all morning. Then they started stomping their feet. "KEP-NER, KEP-NER, KEP-NER!" they shouted.

I couldn't believe it. Was this really happening?

Asher threw me a big grin. So did Dee Dee as she returned to her chair. I mouthed her a silent "thanks."

I think maybe that was one of the sweetest things anyone had ever done for me. I brushed away a leftover tear. I couldn't help it.

Then I saw Traci and Felicia and Dave, on their feet with the rest of the audience.

But what about Arielle?

Slowly I turned to look at my friend. *Was* she my friend still?

Arielle shrugged. Then she gave me a grin—and stood up, too! She started clapping with everyone else.

"Dee Dee's right. You deserve to win, Amanda Panda," she said, coming over to give me a hug. "Congratulations. I concede."

That night Arielle, Felicia, Traci, and I had a celebration sleepover at Traci's house. But we weren't celebrating my becoming sixth-grade president next week. We were celebrating being best friends again.

All four of us.

We threw all of Traci's pillows and couch cushions on the floor of her bedroom, turned up the tunes, and jumped around in our pajamas.

I guess we didn't hear Dave pounding on Traci's door.

"Hey," he said, poking his head in. "Keep it down, will you? I'm trying to study."

"On a Friday night?" Arielle asked. "You can't be serious."

I looked down at my purple pajamas with the stars

and moons on them. Great. Now Dave had caught me looking like a little kid.

Traci threw a pillow at her brother. "He's not studying. He just wanted an excuse to see Amanda."

She and Felicia and Arielle all started making kissy-kissy noises.

"Hey! Knock it off!" Dave said, blushing. He quickly shut the door and left.

"You *guys!*" I protested.

"Guess someone's going to have a date for the big fall dance," Felicia teased.

I laughed. The sixth grade *was* going to sponsor a dance in two weeks—to benefit the WLMS arts program! Arielle and I were organizing it together. We'd already cleared it with the main office. Arielle was getting the DJ.

The first thing I was going to do as president was make Arielle social activities director. It was a newly created position I had come up with, and it seemed tailor-made for Arielle. She was the social queen.

"I'm going to have a date, too," Arielle announced.

We all looked at her, confused.

"Asher Bank?" Felicia guessed.

Arielle shook her head. "Nope," she said. "Tyler Bank. Asher's cousin. They look a lot alike. Except Tyler is in our grade. He goes to Wonder Lake Prep."

"Wow," Traci said.

"That's where Asher's girlfriend goes to school,

too," Arielle went on. "He told me he's bringing her to the dance. So I guess we'll sort of be double-dating."

"Ooooh," I said, nodding. "*I* get it. That's why Asher asked me if you had a boyfriend already." I had told Arielle the whole story after the debate.

"Okay," Felicia said. "So that gives Traci and me two weeks to get dates. Traci, you'll have Ryan Bradley."

Traci blushed. "Come on! I don't know about that."

"And I'll have . . ." Felicia's face fell. "No one, I guess."

"I don't know about that, either," Traci said quickly. "Kevin Johnson keeps staring at you in orchestra. He loses his place in the music about ten times a minute."

"Okay, then, turn up the music!" Arielle said. "I'll show you these cool dance moves from the new Tahira video. I taped it off MTV last night."

Felicia threw a handful of popcorn at her. "Tahira?" she teased. "Who likes *Tahira?*"

"I do," Arielle said. She threw another one of Traci's pillows at her and missed. It hit the wall, sending feathers flying everywhere.

I reached into the bowl on Traci's nightstand and threw M&M's at everyone.

"You *guys!*" Traci protested. "If we make another mess, my mom is going to kill us!"

But it was too late.

Once the four of us best friends start something, there's no stopping us!

142